Graveyards of the Banks
by Nyla Nox

Volume 1
I did it for the money

Cover design by Potamus Studios

First Edition, 2015.
This Edition, 2017.

Athens Publishing
Bangkok, Thailand

ISBN-13: 978-1542617307
ISBN-10: 1542617308

SEVEN SEASONS OF MIDNIGHTS AT THE MOST SUCCESSFUL BANK IN THE UNIVERSE

VOLUME 1 – I DID IT FOR THE MONEY
Season One and Two

VOLUME 2 – MONSTERS ARISING
Season Three, Four and Five

VOLUME 3 – SLAUGHTERHOUSE MORNING
Season Six and Seven

VOLUME 1
I DID IT FOR THE MONEY

Like a space ship, the Most Successful Bank in the Universe had its own climate, self-contained and separate from the city and island it was anchored in.

The air we breathed entered the secret Building Without a Name through huge filters on the roof. Generations upon generations of tiny creatures lived and died in the pipes that pumped this air onto desks and hair and cups of tea. And into our lungs.

Only the fittest of those tiny creatures survived. Bacteria, fungi and assorted particles adapted in a heroic Darwinian effort.

SEASON ONE
I DID IT FOR THE MONEY

I did it for the money

When I walked into the agency, I had three pounds left. I held them tight inside my pocket, two hooked between my fingers, the third pressed into the flesh of my hand.

I had at home two Swiss roll cakes, one already bitten into, the other still untouched. I had prowled the shop for a long time, studying packages. People looked at me knowingly. They probably thought I was on a strict diet, but I was looking for the highest calorie count per penny.

'Finally', said the agent, pulling me through the door of the Georgian mansion behind the Bank of England. She was already in her coat.

Further down the gloomy corridor I saw a few huddled figures.

The agent nodded.

'You're going with them.'

It was almost 7PM. What about business hours?

The agent laughed, but quickly and briefly. We didn't really have time for it.

'Now listen', she said, and reeled off a whole list of arcane instructions. 'For the Test. Keep to what I told you', she said. 'Exactly what I told you! Whatever happens.'

The three pounds in my pocket agreed with her absolutely.

The agent waved to a pale young man in the group.

'Address', she said.

'Peter', said the guy and smiled. 'I'll take care of it.'

The agent looked at us one last time, nodded briefly and left.

There were ten of us. I counted.

While I was calculating the price of the tube ride in my head (I would have taken the bus or even walked but I was going to have to keep up with the group), a woman with asymmetric red hair suggested taking a taxi.

'Oh, yes, it's close. It'll be so much less hassle.' They all agreed.

Maybe it had been rash, buying those Swiss rolls. How would I get home when my three pounds were spent?

A taxi came. People hailed it expertly. They were used to taking taxis. The driver protested but Peter squeezed me into the first one and pulled the door shut. 'The others can follow', he said and smiled again. We raced through the London evening. I was thrown against Peter and the red haired woman who said she was an artist. Maybe she was poor, too?

The taxi knew where the company was, Peter knew where the company was, everybody knew where the company was. I smiled like crazy and tried to remember all the advice that the agent had given me in her coat.

When we arrived, people reached into their pockets and bags. I did too but when I brought out my precious coins,

Peter took only one.

'Is that fair', I asked the young black guy who looked as if he was still a student.

'You'll pay it back next week', said Peter.

Next week? That would mean we would all get through, I thought.

Peter nodded. He was so confident.

When I climbed out, we were standing in front of a graveyard. Tombstones and memorial tablets dating back to the time of the Great Plague huddled together in the city shadows. This was where we were going?

Peter expertly led the way through the gravestones to a building rising recklessly above the centuries of dead. There was no name, no logo on the wall, no indication that anything was here except darkness.

As we got closer, I could see a small nondescript door.

The red haired woman hit a discreetly placed button. We waited and a buzz came back. The small nondescript door gave to Peter's touch and we went in. It closed behind us without a sound. Before us stretched a long bleak corridor. There was only one direction to go, so we followed it. We were inside.

As my eyes got used to the darkness, I could see a brighter gloom ahead. We turned the corner into a much wider entrance, surrounded by guards and drivers in uniform. The people in my new peer group didn't know as much as they thought about this place. They were outsiders, just like me, and so, like me, they had to walk through the dark corridor.

As we joined the main hall, the ceiling soared to a head spinning height. The floor now sparkled in marble. The walls were clad in metal.

All these shiny reflections made me feel a little dizzy. Maybe I should have taken one of the Swiss Rolls with me, scrunched up inside my pocket. But then what would I eat when I got home?

Maybe they would offer us coffee. Then I could put in lots of sugar. And full fat milk, if they had it. Although it would mean alienating the women in the group.

The hall was completely empty, emphasising the stark design. This was a place of no nonsense. We walked between the metal walls, covering the considerable distance to the front desk. My reflection flickered in the marble. Breathing became a challenge.

The desk was huge, all metal. The guards behind it exuded suspicion. Peter took charge. He had a name from the agent that would let us in. The guards doubted it. Delays and misdirections. I tried to breathe right but I started to get dizzy again. There was nowhere to sit down. As we waited, the guys joked. The artist tried to steer the conversation towards her paintings. I held onto the desk, hiding my shaking hands. I noticed there were no windows.

Reluctantly, and in exchange for our IDs, the guards gave us large white tags that said 'GUEST'. I clipped mine to my coat. Everyone could see I was not an enemy. Other people just slipped them into their pockets.

Some more waiting, some more jokes, some more deep breaths, and then our guide appeared.

She was very well dressed and made up in pastel colours, 'groomed' all over. Probably not much older than me but altogether from a different plane of existence. No one could ever imagine her just with three pounds in her pocket. Well, two now, actually.

She spoke very quietly, so that we had to crowd around her, and even then she didn't say much. Just to follow her. I may have missed the hello.

Behind the desk, the steel walls rose to enclose a ledge that looked a bit like a launching pad for small spaceships. Up to that ledge led a pair of escalators. Stairs were not enough for this company.

I was glad about the escalators. I could rest my shaking knees.

Up on the metal ledge, we waited for the lifts. Our guide pressed all the buttons and was muttering about the slowness of the service. She really worked here. That was clear. She had enough seniority to complain about the lifts.

We entered the small metal cabin. I expected to go up, but we went down. And down again.

'Yes', said the guide. 'We are going to the Third Basement.'

What is going on here?

The organisation I was about to join was of course supremely legal. I knew that. If it broke any laws it has never been prosecuted, let alone convicted. The agent had hinted that it was the most powerful organisation in the world.

My first impressions of the organisation reflected its self-image: dominant, intimidating, and shrouded in mystery. A place so secret that it didn't even have its name on the door... I had never heard of such a place. But if all went well, I was destined to become one of the very few not only to see its hidden walls but actually live inside them. I, of all people, would see what this organisation was truly like. I felt dizzy again.

Right then I was on my way down to its very bowels, the Third Basement far below the shiny marble halls. This is where a crucial procedure would be initiated: the selection of the fittest. And in this organisation, only the fittest survived. I knew that, too.

Selection of the Fittest in the Third Basement

The lift announced it: Third Basement. This was where our future would be decided.

I nearly collapsed with the thought of all the massive concrete above. But then I thought, no, no, it was safe. Surely, this company was always safe, even deep down in the earth. The doors opened on a dim, humid passage way. The walls were raw and unpainted. The floor had some kind of carpet strip along the middle that tripped the red-haired artist up immediately. Untidy heaps of storage boxes and cables snaking in from points unknown threatened to block our passage.

I knew I would never find my way out of here on my own.

At some point, the corridor opened out onto a small corner with nowhere to go.

'That's the kitchen', said our guide. 'You better get what you need now, it's a long way to the Testing Room.'

The artist was straight in and the young guy not far behind. Peter joked and allowed the rest of us to go first. He wasn't too worried about losing a bit of time. Everyone had tea but I needed coffee. I failed to find it and had to ask for help. The artist lost her patience. Was I already a drain on the team? I tried not to spill the hot water and offered sugar packs around.

Then took a sip while we were walking, spilling a little on the way. Peter and the other guys carried two cups each. Why hadn't I thought of that?

I hurried to catch up with the group, the artist's voice a homing signal through the convoluted concrete corridors. At some point, a door was half open, showing a loading bay. Did the armoured trucks come down this far? Was there a private connection with the underground system? Anything seemed possible.

Three workmen passed in silence.

The final corridor, abruptly leading to nothing, had three doors set in the wall. Our guide disappeared into the middle one. It was thick and heavy, so that we had to put our shoulders to it. The walls were a metre thick. If the world was blown up in a nuclear disaster during the selection procedure, we would be alive to re-populate it.

I told myself to focus.

Inside the door cold light shone on thinly painted walls, and on rows of metal desks with computer terminals, a teacher's platform and a whiteboard at the front.

We were asked to spread out, one to a row, spaced apart so we couldn't see each other's monitors. We did as told. I put my coffee on the desk, drank deeply, and felt the hot sugar rush through my system. Our guide introduced herself. I didn't catch exactly what she was, the Head of something. I hoped she got enough vitamin D down here.

Then it was time for the Test.

There are many ways to arrange selection of the fittest, and this was the one for us.

This test was what the agent in her coat had tried to prepare us for. It was rumoured to be the toughest test in town (of its kind) and designed to fail as many people as possible. The selection was 'rigorous'. Now I know what they mean whenever that word crops up.

For me, the Test (it loomed so large it was burning a T shape into my mind) felt like my last chance. I didn't know how the other nine felt. How many would get through? I was terrified.

The Test lasted two hours, or maybe three or four, by the reckoning of my internal clock.

I took one look at the screen, and went into freefall. Desperately, I tried to remember the agent's instructions.

There were problems here I hadn't even known existed, and I had no hope of finding out what they were, let alone solve them. Peter felt free to ask a few questions and to my extreme surprise he was answered. I just followed my instincts, since there was nothing else.

The Head sat down at the back of the room 'where I can

see you'.

I immersed myself more deeply in the Test. The chart was very, very difficult, much more difficult than even the agent had foretold. Was that a trap?

I solved it. I doubted myself. I made mistakes. I corrected them and made new ones.

And was that drawing really as easy as it looked? Peter didn't ask any more questions so I assumed he knew. Or had I missed something here? I remembered when I failed a translation test in school at the age of ten because I had overlooked one whole sentence. How my mother had screamed. How I had crawled away, ready to die of shame.

My coffee ran low. There was no sugar and there was no hope.

I tried to proof everything many times, as the Head kept telling us. Both she and the agent were very strict on that. In fact, if I got the proofreading wrong I would be failed.

Unfortunately, I had never proofread anything before. I tried very hard to focus.

Time was still left. I doubted again. I went back to my chart and gave it all sorts of extras, all the things that I had ever learned. What people call 'Bells and Whistles' but that expression seemed frivolous here.

Surreptitiously I checked on my two pounds. I still had them. Both.

People left. Peter left, joking with the Head. The artist left. Everybody left. I decided to stay as long as possible.

Only me and the Head now. I checked my work one last time and then returned the Test one minute before official closing.

The Head didn't say a thing, just nodded. I took my empty coffee cup and my coat, and pushed through the heavy door. My bones could not stay. My legs started walking. I had no idea where I was. The workmen had disappeared, but the scattered debris was still there. I think I passed the door to the landing bay but it was closed.

I kept walking. And then I ran across the young guy, also wandering around although he had finished much earlier. Together we managed to locate the lift.

That was lucky but it was also unlucky because I had hoped to take another sugary coffee from the kitchen. And a fistful of sachets. Now I couldn't.

We came out on the launch pad for space ships. It glittered like a thousand diamonds after our time down in the Third Basement.

'I'm scared', said the young guy. 'I've been out of work for so long…'

Maybe I could have taken the coffee after all.

The guards had to run after us for our GUEST tags. What if we had carried them out into the street? Well, we are all but guests upon this earth, I thought. That was another effect of this place – it really put you in touch with your mortality.

I didn't know the buses around here. And buses don't like the city of London when it is late. They run very fast, down the emptying roads. It took me some time until I was bold enough to stop one of them.

The last leg of the journey home, walking to my flat, was hard. My legs didn't want to push into the pavement. But the thought of my Swiss rolls sustained me.

Outside my building my next door neighbour was fumbling drunkenly with his car keys. We nodded at each other and I escaped into my bedsit ahead of his heavy steps. A few minutes later I inhaled the fumes from his warmed up dinner wafting through the kitchen partition. I hoped the twice burnt fish gave him comfort. I had no idea how he spent his days.

We would hear soon, the agent had said. Not from the company, of course, who could and would not converse with us directly on such matters, but from her.

I checked that my voicemail worked. I checked my email. I checked everything twice. And then once again.

Then I unwrapped my half bitten Swiss roll. I sank my teeth into the sweet, deep, rich dark tissue, and closed my mouth around the swirls of sticky filling. I fell asleep fully dressed, clutching the cake in my fingers.

My landlady didn't know I was out of work.

I dreamed of beautiful landscapes and swimming in an endless sea, warm and happy, and free to move in all the blue directions.

Subject and object

When I woke, my eyes went, as always, to my book shelves. Askew and slowly sliding into the wide empty gaps were my old project files. My books had been sold long ago, but the files were worth nothing. They were only the essence of my life, and my passion.

Of course, I had brought this on entirely myself. I had insisted on studying the humanities, and practised my choice, anthropology, as much as I could afford to. I had been warned that it was a field that tolerated only the very rich and the very lucky. I had seen the statistics. But had I listened? No, I had only listened to my own heart.

It had been my dream, or I thought my vocation in life, to observe and analyse people and cultures. For many years, I searched for patterns and tried to find the big overview.

Except that I couldn't afford it. Not after I stopped being a student. Not after the end of my first professional project which was inadequately paid, or the end of the penultimate one which I paid for myself. And definitely not after the end of the very last project of all which took whatever I could borrow, and couldn't pay back, in spite of doing as much as possible myself, including the layout and graphics, a steep and frustrating learning curve. Not after those many months without work, and the Era of the Swiss Roll.

All I could afford now was to be the object of anthropology.

The call

The call came on my second day of waiting, early in the afternoon. I had heard my neighbours walk down the stairs from their bedsits in the morning, and then, more slowly, back up again at night. Then the TVs through the walls. Then the faint sounds of mammals in bed. For two days I watched the sun shift shadows through the window, trying to re-read a favourite science fiction novel from the almost empty shelf behind me. At times like these, I like to be far from earth.

The agent introduced herself by first name only which confused me a little. She was not a friend. But, she explained, she had to do this in case I was working elsewhere and needed to be headhunted.

Head hunted! Visions of beautifully suited executives danced across my mind.

I waited for her verdict.

'Well you've passed the Test', she said, irritated. 'Three weeks in the Third Basement, 4PM to midnight, starting today.'

The Most Successful Bank in the Universe

The company I had just managed to find employment (or more accurately an entry slot for further selection towards that employment) with was, of course, the Most Successful Bank in the Universe.

This Bank was famous and powerful long before I ever heard of it, and many people wished nothing more than to work in this Bank.

I didn't know that. I didn't even know much about the Bank itself, not even what kind of banking it did, why it didn't have any branches you could open an account in, and what it was that made it so famous and desirable above all other Banks.

The only person I had consulted, briefly, was the father of an old school friend who worked at another, lesser bank in the city. His face lit up first with admiration, then envy, then admiration again. 'Of course', he said, 'it's the gold standard. If you can get in there, in any capacity…' He looked out the window as if to contemplate the vast opportunities offered at the Most Successful Bank in the Universe which he, of course, had never had a chance to explore himself. My school friend gave me a sharp glance. I had made her father very uncomfortable. That was bad news for the family…

But it made little difference in my decision to accept the job. Like many students of the humanities, I had almost prided myself on my ignorance of matters of commerce. I certainly wasn't going to be impressed by a bank. Even if it was a Bank.

I only looked at the hourly rates the agency promised, particularly on the night shift. I had never earned so much money before. Granted, the skills they were asking for had nothing to do with my education and previous work experience, but I had acquired most of them the hard way, doing every supporting task I could do myself in the course of my now defunct projects so that I didn't have to pay someone else with money I didn't have. I had never really valued those lesser skills, but now they were the ones that kept me alive while my higher skills had managed to accumulate nothing for me but debt.

Listening to some of my friends talking disdainfully about the banking industry I kept quiet. Was this job a betrayal? And if so, of what?

One look at my bank account (with the kind of bank that did have local branches!) convinced me that I had to at least try. And anyway, my friends were not bankers, nor did they know any, apart from that one Dad. When I tried to read up on it, I didn't find a lot of concrete information about what it was actually like to work inside the Building Without a Name. I couldn't even google any pictures of the working floors. It seemed that the very chairs and desks were confidential. And indeed, I did find out later that the taking of photographs was strictly forbidden. A rule that was relentlessly enforced, like all the minor rules in the Bank. Every aspect of life in the Most Successful Bank in the Universe was shrouded in mystery and hidden behind generic superlatives. I suppose I could have wondered why…

Well, I told myself, this was an opportunity to find out for myself. I would know something that none of my friends would know. They were all working in academics, education, the arts, or even the public sector, said to be unproductive and doomed to fail. From the perspective of the Bank, they were far removed from where the sausage was made. Or, in this case, the money.

Maybe I, too, would learn how to be efficient and successful, like the Bank.

But the fact remains that, unlike the bankers who prepared, competed and aspired all their lives to join it, I stumbled right into the heart of the Most Successful Bank in the Universe inadvertently and almost by accident.

Basic Training: my core group

In the military, people hark back forever to their original training group. Sometimes it fuses into a power cell propelling stellar careers. Sometimes brothers in arms marry into each other's families. Sometimes, decades later, the trainees become generals and stage a coup, making each other wealthy dictators.

The seven people who assembled in the Third Basement the next day did nothing to inspire such lifelong fealty.

I recognised the red haired artist (Rita) and the young guy (Julian, we were now telling each other names) from my Test, and, of course, as he had so confidently predicted, Peter. There were three others, survivors of a selection group of twelve, several weeks ago. Again, I was lucky.

As it turned out, very lucky indeed. I had been told, by the Head herself, on the phone, that my Test contained several proofing mistakes. 'Usually, when people make a proofing mistake, I fail them', she said, with the cold assurance of someone who is paid to fail people on a daily basis.

I tried not to breathe heavily into my phone. Had the agent made a mistake? Had I hoped just to be disappointed?

'But', said the Head, 'yours is the best technical Test I've ever seen.'

Of course I didn't know how long 'ever' was but the Head had looked to me like someone who had held a long tenure. (At the time I was blissfully unaware of the average length of tenure at that company…) I should have felt proud of myself, or at least happy, but I was too shocked from my near-miss.

'So you passed', she said. I wish I had had such luck in anthropology.

'Sorry', I said, and, 'thank you.'

'I've told the Trainer you need to be watched', said the Head and hung up.

And, the training was paid. The agent told me. Not very well, but paid. Whereas in my previous field….

Money! At the end of the week. At the end of THIS week!

It had been such a long time since my last pay check, I wasn't sure I remembered the procedure. But I hoped it would cover my rent, and the buses, and the makings of sandwiches at home.

If I survived the training, I would earn a good hourly wage. And even more if I got onto the night shift, my goal right from the start. The agent had told me I would. But who knew?

It was a long way in the future, anyway.

At the moment, we were stuck in the tea corner of the Third Basement. Damp, dark and surrounded by metre thick concrete on five sides (it was tucked between various competing dead ends), this was not a place where you would want to linger, except of course if the only alternative was the Training Room. Besides, coffee, sugar and real milk from a fridge were Bank benefits that we were already entitled to enjoy. Tax free.

I didn't know if the others were all as desperate as I was. But I was absolutely determined to succeed. I would work on my weaknesses and develop my strengths. From now on I would double and triple check my copying and proof reading.

From now on I would make sure I wouldn't be caught out again and almost not get the job. From now on I would be sensible and abandon my dreams.

Really.

We stocked up. Everyone was carrying two drinks now and I was already used to the splash burns on my hands. I decided to look at it as a way of warming up for a freezing shift inside the bunker walls.

Rita, the artist, was well ahead of me. As on the day of the Test, she wore a long men's shirt over leggings, very different from the usual banking attire, even down here in 'smart casual' land. I felt frumpy next to her. And I never managed to catch up, somehow. I had hoped we could maybe become friends, or buddies at least, but she hardly even looked at me except on the occasions when she corrected some of my opinions on art history.

'Just wait', said the Trainer, a man who always wore a suit although it was not mandatory down here, 'it's even colder on the Seventh Floor.'

The Seventh Floor. That was the place to be. If we made it there….

Access to the Seventh Floor was through continuous assessment, by him, and selection would be 'rigorous'. I looked around, and so did Peter. Less than 30 percent had made it here from each test group. It crossed my mind that there might be a fail quota.

The Trainer announced a ten minute break. We took it, grumbling to each other that it wasn't really long enough since the walk to the tea corner took up a considerable slice of that time. We really had no idea…

The Center of Global Excellence

So what was it that fulfilled such a vital function at the Bank that we were being recruited, selected, tested, trained and tested again (rigorously, of course!) until only the fittest remained, and then trained again for weeks at the expense of the company (however close to the minimum wage)?

'Well', said the Trainer, sitting behind his desk on the raised platform, 'the first thing you have to remember is that we are a Center of Global Excellence.'

And then, when we showed no reaction, 'that means, we are the best of our kind.'

Peter obliged.

'In London?'

The Trainer allowed himself a thin smile.

'No. In the world.'

We managed a few little ohs and ahs. I had no idea what any of this meant.

'And the bankers need us, 24/7, 365 days a year. For the Books. We are essential to the Bank.'

That was good to hear, I thought.

We were all here because we were hoping to join the Bank's 'Graphics Center', a 24/7 operation that produced Books for pitches, deals, mergers and acquisitions, and various advisory functions, used mainly, but not exclusively, by the Bank's Investment Banking division. This was not a decorative extra. The Books were the only tangible object that the Bank's clients ever held in their hands, in return for the astronomic fees they paid. Of course they expected Global Excellence, and we were here to provide it.

Every day, highly sensitive information from everywhere in the Bank passed through the Center. It was right at the heart of it all. If selected, we, a random group of people who had never aspired to joining it, would become the ultimate carriers of the Bank's secrets.

When I looked around I realised that, just like me, most people were not graphics professionals but came from a diversity of backgrounds where we had acquired the necessary skills. And we did have those skills in abundance, I could see that when I sneaked a look at my neighbours' screens. The 'highly competitive test' that had been administered to us, right here, down in the Third Basement, by the Head of Training, had indeed selected a skilled workforce, and maybe the seven of us were indeed the Best and Fittest in our field.. So what did we need to learn? According to the Trainer in a Suit, the purpose of Basic Training in the Third Basement was to teach us the 'best practices' developed by the Bank's Graphics Department, and its complex house style.

But nothing was ever quite what it seemed at the Most Successful Bank in the Universe...

'Well, back to work', said the Trainer.

We bent our heads and obeyed.

Nothing further was ever explained to us. Not the context of the Graphics Center within the company and certainly not the structure, mission or purpose of the Most Successful Bank in the Universe itself. Like our ice cold Trainer, the Bank parted with information very reluctantly, as if it they were giving away an advantage. We were reduced to making our own observations and extrapolated from whatever we could.

So far, what I knew was this: we were learning to produce something that was called 'The Page'.

The Page was laid out according to various intricate rules. It contained text and illustrations, including many kinds of charts, diagrams, pictures and maps. While the bankers provided the content, it was our job to create the visuals. All the documents that left the Bank to meet the universe outside were formatted to a brand specific design, including company colours, fonts, layout and other graphics elements.

These so-called 'house styles' were written down in a bible not unlike the sacred book of a salvation religion. They proclaimed the rules on everything from paragraph spacings to chart colour sequences, line thickness and complex layout proportions. Nothing could go out that broke these rules.

It was like learning a whole new and very difficult language, like a combination of fifth century Mandarin and nineteenth century German.

I understood the need for consistency and an overall company look. I tried to absorb the design philosophy. I extended my mind in previously unexplored directions. I diligently practiced the extremely fine motor skills needed to control my mouse in complex illustrations.

'Not everyone will make it through Basic Training', said Peter to his desk mate Ilya from the other test group, who nodded wisely. Ilya was already well tuned into rumour…

Week Two in the Third Basement and one of us had already been eliminated. We could all see that the workspace next to Julian was empty, but it was never mentioned.

I settled down to my learning task of the evening. One quarter of the Page I was trying to create was a so-called 'combination chart'. These charts were a lot like unruly animals, always trying to run away in a different directions. The bankers, said the Trainer, really liked combination charts but… He hinted at dark practices aimed at circumventing the company guidelines. Then he permitted himself a little smile.

I looked at my chart. It was quite successful I felt. Maybe I did have a talent for this. As for gathering information on the Bank, one thing I had already noticed. The curves always went upwards.

Another quarter of the Page layout had to be filled with an enormous amount of text. How could I do that and still fulfil all the regulations? There were very specific rules about the relationship between font size and paragraph spacing that must not be broken. I tried to follow them all and ended up with a horrible cluster of tiny lines and a lot of white space. The Trainer's eyes rested on me while I got more and more anxious. Yes, it was only a page. But it was a Page that might well decide my fate…

The Trainer walked through the rows, people looking up to him.

He gave out judgment.

When he got to Julian who was sitting right behind me, he turned his monitor around so that we could all see. I was appalled to realise I was staring into a rough copy of my own beautiful chart.

'What is this', said the Trainer to the class.

'A combination chart', I heard myself say.

The Trainer looked at me with suspicion.

'There's something missing', he said.

Our class looked around all over the chart, now enlarged to fill the entire screen. Julian looked too, craning his neck.

'I don't know', he said, defeated.

A giggle flashed from the front row where Rita sat. She already had a friend, not me but a well dressed woman from the other group who seemed to excel at pleasing our Trainer.

The Trainer pointed to the value axis of the chart. It went from 0 to 500, and I thought it was beautifully proportioned, just like mine.

'What?' said the Trainer, 'What?' striking the monitor with his pen.

The giggles flared up again. I had no idea what he was asking for. Julian looked around helplessly.

'Read it.'

'0 to 500', he read out, as quietly as he could.

'What?' repeated the Trainer, much louder now, '500 what????'

Julian didn't know.

'Exactly', said the Trainer. '500 dollars?'

Even I knew that couldn't be right. 500 dollars wasn't worth setting up a chart for.

The Trainer struck the monitor again. It gave a hard, menacing sound.

'500 BILLION dollars', he said. 'Put it in!'

Trembling, Julian reached for his mouse and made space for the value axis title.

'$ bn' it said now. I quietly made the same adjustment.

Finally, the Trainer lost his patience. He reached for Julian's mouse and grabbed it, hard. Julian gave a little sound like a very surprised rabbit which elicited a huge volley of giggles from the front row.

The Trainer gave Julian an angry look and, in one fell, highly skilled swoop, took out the space between $ and bn.

'Never, never a space in between', he shouted. 'Never, never a space in between. Between the dollar and the billion.'

And there never was.

I admit I was shocked. I hadn't heard anyone talk like this since I left school. Even then, no one had ever spoken to an *adult* like this. People had been unpleasant, snarky, nasty, yes. But not this brutal show of power, this coerced submission.

But the Trainer was not finished. Oh no.

He moved over to me. But instead of my now perfect chart, he focused on the miserable looking text.

'I tried to follow all the rules', I said. My voice sounded suspiciously like another rabbit. What hunts rabbits? Maybe a feral dog? Maybe a falcon from Hyde Park? Maybe a weasel?

The Trainer looked at me.

'You', he said, 'are not a very visual person. No potential for creativity at all. I've noticed that before. Break.'

Satisfied, the Trainer went back to his elevated platform and unwrapped his sandwich. It was from a gourmet shop.

I sat there for a few moments, losing valuable tea brewing time, while everyone else stampeded through the concrete warrens.

A memory flashed into my mind. Myself, at age 12 or so, in a large schoolroom, watching in petrified horror as my maths teacher lifted the back flap of my exercise book, high up in the air, revealing that it was not a proper exercise book at all but a bundle of pages saved over from other exercise books and taped together at the back, the result of what I had thought of as an ingenious way to prolong its life and avoid the dreaded task of asking my mother to buy a me new one. I knew very well that there was never a good moment in the household finances for such a purchase. My maths teacher, I hope to God, was ignorant of this fact. The class joined him in uproarious laughter. The taped pages hung down from his upstretched hand like a dismembered accordion.

My face burned hot with shame. I didn't want that memory but it had found a hook. Again, what hunts rabbits?

I managed to get up and rush towards the Basement kitchen, desperately swallowing back the tears.

'The Trainer is S&I', said Peter. He and Ilya were leaning against the cupboards in the kitchen corner, pushing the drawers in and out. They seemed remarkably relaxed and I had noticed that they always had their work finished ahead of everyone else. Peter was clearly very good at making useful alliances. His new friend used to be a lawyer back in Russia before he settled in London.

'S&I', I asked. I didn't mind taking the bait. I was going to do whatever it took to avoid making more mistakes.

Peter and Ilya exchanged a conspiratorial glance.

'Upstairs', Peter said.

'On every floor', added Ilya.

'They know everything. And they constantly look over your shoulder. They only report to each other. And New York. Never cross them.'

If they hoped I would be properly impressed they were right. I nodded and had to switch the kettle back on again since I had missed the boiling. For a moment I wondered what pipes the water had run through before it reached the Third Basement and how often this particular water had boiled already. Then I dunked my tea bag.

'What's S&I stand for?' I said.

'Oh, I don't know', said Ilya, flexing his right hand. 'There's some kind of strange feeling in my fingers…'

'Mine too', I said. 'I burned them.'

'Serve and Inform', said Peter proudly, 'Serve and Inform.'

Rita breezed down the corridor back to the Training Room with her new best friend, kicking cartons and raising echoes of the infantry. The friend, ex tele-marketing, already knew the right people upstairs, or so she said, and was going to make a career out of this. Hanging back, I was overtaken by Julian.

'Hi', I said, uncertainly.

'Oh hi', he said. 'Did you get a call from the agent today?'

Another call from the agent? What else had I missed?

'Yeah', said Julian. 'Got a call from the agency just now saying that I wasn't up to shape. They're on my case. I have to be faster.'

He shook his head.

I shook my head too but didn't know what to say.

When we got to the room and passed through the metre thick walls, the class had started. Rita and her friend sat in the first row and were listening diligently to the Trainer's directions.

Why didn't you leave?

At this early stage, maybe I could have.

So why did I persevere with something so stressful and degrading, why did I not walk out proudly into the sunlight (or, in this case, the polluted evening drizzle over the City of London)?

Well, I had already done that. For most of my life I had proudly done what I felt called to do. Now, I was paying the price. The painful treatment in the Third Basement only re-enforced my even more painful awareness of the desperate financial situation I was in, atonement for all my years of trying to create a life in the humanities.

And, even this early on, eight hours per evening of that kind of Training had started to infiltrate my mind. I had already begun to accept it as the inevitable, the place I went to every night, the place I would go to for the foreseeable future. My place in life.

Of course, I never would have said that, or allowed it as a fully conscious thought. I expended considerable energy trying not to become too aware of what was happening inside myself.

But, when Peter said, during Week Three in the five sided tea corner of the Third Basement, 'We wouldn't be here if we didn't want to be here', I felt he was stating a painful truth. If I had left, dozens would have jumped at the chance to replace me.

And, if I survived to ascend to the Seventh Floor, I would make more money that I ever had before. Not as much as a banker, but more than the head teacher of a primary school. More than my whole team of anthropologists clumped together.

Life is pain. Might as well get paid for it...

Peter and the tombstone

Once again I had miscalculated the time it took the three buses to get to the Bank. Today I was far too early.

Two doors down from the bus stop was a trendy coffee shop. Through the window I could see a red sofa under a golden picture frame. It was empty and I wanted to go and sit there.

One look at the prices displayed behind the coffee counter made it clear to me that this was still way out of my range.

Luckily, the graveyard was even closer.

I walked through the low gate and was surrounded by tombs and sunken stones. If there had ever been a church it was now long gone, abandoning the graves on the time line to eternity. Maybe it was the centuries of acid rain or maybe it was a parish requirement, but the slabs all had a washed out ivory tint, not unlike the colour of old bones, long after the flesh has fallen away.

I found a tomb in the shape of a marble box, engraved all round and on the top with the details of the departed. I sat down on it and took out my book. I was still on far future science fiction.

The afternoon was fading, and the shadow of the Bank fell over me and my marble resting place.

I knew I had my home made sandwich with me, and after a short but futile struggle I wrestled it out of my bag to eat it all at once. A fine drizzle settled in and coated the pages of my book.

I had just managed to transport myself out to a fantastical alien planet when I heard a voice saying my name.

Although there was a path somewhere down the graveyard, the tombstones were set among the fertile grass that swallowed all footsteps. The voice was very close.

'Nyla.'

The alien planet shattered in my imagination. I looked up. And into Peter's smile.

'Your favourite gravestone?' he said.

I looked over at the anonymous entrance.

'Yes', I said. 'It's fairly comfortable, as gravestones go.'

Peter broke out into a boyish grin.

'I like to sit on them too', he said. 'Maybe not polite, considering what's underneath, but I'm sure they don't mind. Can I join you?'

I moved over on the tombstone. My thighs met the fresh cold of marble that has not been sat on for a long time.

Peter perched at the edge, supporting himself by stretching out his long legs into the grass. I could see the outline of some nice, firm muscle under his dark pants.

'What are you having?' he said companionably.

I had forgotten the half eaten sandwich in my hand. Now I wished I had dropped it behind the grave. It was just a pitiful thing, margarine and scrapes of old cheese.

Luckily, Peter didn't really want to know.

He held up his long red paper cup and smiled some more.

'I really love this stuff', he said. I noticed it bore the logo from the trendy coffee shop.

I knew what Peter earned. The same as me. I wondered how he could afford this. Of course it was the last thing I could ask.

We sat and chatted for a while. I wasn't sure how I rated my chances of passing the Training. As always, Peter was confident.

'They've invested in us', he said. 'And anyway, you're good at this.'

I hoped he was right.

Then the drizzle turned into heavy rain and drove us in.

My book was soaked at the edges, but I managed to slip it into my bag together with the margarine sandwich while Peter was focusing on the last sips of his gourmet coffee.

For a moment I thought he was going to toss the cup over the tomb, deeper into the graveyard towards the looming evening. I must have looked a little shocked, because he grinned again and tamely carried it in.

'Oh', he said, walking down the dark corridor with me, 'I almost forgot: philosophy.'

'Anthropology', I said. He nodded.

Philosophy! He must have known he where he would end up, sooner or later.

The Room with Four Windows on the Night

'Well', said the Trainer wearily, 'next week most of you will be up on the Seventh Floor.' In a rare display of common human decency, most of us tried not to look in Julian's direction. Rita and her well connected tele-marketing neighbour were not so afflicted. They stared openly.

'So', I said bravely, 'what is it like?'

'Oh, it's ok', said the Trainer dismissively. 'It's a great team up there. We are a Center of Global Excellence.'

'And if we have a difficult problem, we can ask S&I', said Ilya.

I held my breath. This was getting close to dangerous territory.

'Yes', said the Trainer evenly, 'you can. We are here to Serve and Inform.'

There was a brief silence as we contemplated the possible implications of this statement.

'What is the room like', said Peter, trying to extend the chat break a little.

The Trainer paused. That was not a question on his list.

'Nice, I suppose', he said. 'The desks are a bit small and sometimes there's not enough space so some of the operators have to sit in Overflow…'

'I have heard', said Peter with an ingratiating smile, 'that the Seventh Floor has windows on all four sides and you can see the whole city of London, the Thames, the Westend and even the Houses of Parliament on a bright morning.'

And the sunrise behind St Paul's, I thought but said nothing. It was hard to imagine down in the Third Basement, but if true, I was looking forward to it.

'Oh', said the Trainer. 'Oh, that. Yes. I suppose so. You don't really notice it much.'

How could you not notice the sunrise behind St Paul's? I'd seen pictures of the view over London, taken from millionaires' penthouse suites. Until now it had not occurred to me that this might be one of the perks of my future job. Maybe I had been getting too negative here.

'And in the daytime the light gets really annoying. Reflections on your screen. People usually pull the blinds.'

But then they couldn't see…

'You will be observed and evaluated all the time, every shift', said the Trainer, retreating to happier grounds. 'If you pass Basic Training. You will get a call.'

Ignorance

And really, I thought, riding the bus back through the earliest hour of midnight, we had learned a lot. The bag rattling on my lap with every pothole was swollen with the Bank's style bible and while I could not claim that I was yet firmly familiar with scripture, I felt I had a good grasp on basic procedures. Silently, I memorised the sequence of the company colours and repeated the Trainer's warnings against the most egregious style sins, such as hairline grids and shadowed fonts. I was now able to see these things with a graphics person's mind set, something that I would never lose again.

But although I had learned so much about the graphics side, the one thing that had been completely lacking in our training was any kind of information about what it actually was that we were doing.

What were those charts for? What did those diagrams illustrate? Why were the pages with standard information set up the way they were?

In other words, what exactly was the business of the Bank?

During our weeks of Basic Training down in the Third Basement, we had been so busy absorbing new information and practising new skills, we had been under so much pressure to pass the test of continuous assessment and please the Trainer in a Suit, that it dawned on me only now, looking out the rain streaked windows of the bus, that I didn't know much more about the Most Successful Bank in the Universe than when I first was tested.

It seemed a little strange, but, I thought, maybe we would get more information later, when we were working 'live' on the Seventh Floor. After all, the more we knew the better we could support the work of the bankers.

The bus was very fast tonight, raising and splashing through fountains of dirty road water. I stuffed my style bible back into the bag and tottered to the door. If I didn't press the stop button well in time, the driver would pass my stop. With high speed. And, in my tired imagination, with glee. Typical public sector employee, I thought.

Even if we hadn't been taught anything about the Bank, I must have already absorbed some of its attitude through my skin.

The call

The next day I got a phone call from the agent, telling me that I would be on the graveyard shift Thursday to Sunday, midnight to eight. It was the best paid shift, especially Saturday and Sunday.

Once again it seemed that my progress at the Most Successful Bank in the Universe would be blessed with the kind of luck that I had never found in my chosen profession.

I breathed out and collapsed on my bed.

Life was so precarious.

Ilya, the former Russian lawyer, was on the late evening shift. Peter (philosophy) and Rita (art) were on the graveyard shift Monday to Friday. Julian, media studies, didn't make it. I have no idea what happened to him. The tele-marketer with connections got a morning shift, less well paid but close to management.

Inside the fortress of the Bank, small hearts were beating, each aflutter on its own.

This was the way it was when I came up to the Seventh Floor.

Coming up from the Basement

On the first Thursday of my shift above, I tried to sleep as much as possible during the day. But I discovered that I couldn't just switch my rhythm around by pure will power. The more I tried to sleep, the more alert I got. At 8PM I finally gave up. And promptly felt incredibly tired, so that I had to drag myself out of bed through pure determination, and stay out. At 9PM I tried to have breakfast but found that my stomach had closed up. My body was nervous before I my feelings let me know. At 10PM I crept under the shower. I used extra deodorant and mouthwash. Then I put on my best blue suit from two seasons ago, with pantyhose intact in all the right places, and marched through the night to catch my bus. It got stuck in the after-pub traffic. I should have known that. Tomorrow I would know better. Meanwhile it was tonight, my first night up on the Seventh Floor, and I was in danger of being late. My stomach clenched itself into a harder ball. The clock was seven minutes shy of midnight when I finally slipped through the hidden door at the back of the graveyard and entered the Building Without a Name.

Then through the dark narrow passage, traversing the shiny steel clad halls with my new company pass, and, finally, up to the Seventh Floor.

Seventh Floor, land of glory, object of desire down in the Third Basement. I had no idea then how well I was going to get to know the Seventh Floor, nor what life there really turned out to be.

The Seventh Floor, far from being a slice of the promised land, revealed itself all too soon as a place of terror and abandonment of all hope. Its icy fingers would creep into my mind, and from there into the rest of my life until I was unable to live, and unable to leave. I often dream of it still.

If I had known… If I had known I would still have gone up to the Seventh Floor. Because, remember, I did it for the money. And for my sins…

And now I was going to see what no human eye was

permitted to glimpse, unless the owner of that eye had a company pass, and made it through the whole phalanx of Tests, Trainings and Secret Background Checks. The inside of a working floor at the Most Successful Bank in the Universe.

I was prepared for awe, but unfortunately I was pressed for time.

The first thing I noticed, even in a hurry, was its size. The Seventh Floor, like most of the Bank's Working Floors, was a huge open space running all around the central elevator block and the toilets which were located outside the security area and could only be reached through impermeable glass doors and with the aid of that all-important company pass. That first night, however, I failed to understand the significance of this architectural feature that would dominate my life on every shift and end up causing permanent physical damage in me and many of my colleagues. Once inside, everything was workspace. And when I say everything, I mean... everything.

The desks (perfectly ordinary office desks in the popular L shape, such as I and the reader will have seen many times in other, less confidential spaces), as far as the eye could see, were arranged in symmetrical groups of four, each group of four L shapes pushed together forming the figure of a cross. It made the entire floor look like a vast modern cemetery seen from a dramatically foreshortened perspective. The bankers never seemed to notice this, but maybe that's why they were bankers and I worked in the graphics centre.

The cross shaped desk groups were crammed in together so closely that there was no path between them. I needed to make it across the field of desks to reach the entrance of the Global Center of Excellence on the other side. But how? Not only were the desks too close, they were also overloaded with paperwork, books and personal belongings that spilled out onto the floor all around them. Anyone who traversed this space (as hundreds of people did every day) had to pick their way across this obstacle course. And back again.

Since nobody was there to help me, and since time was

short, I decided to make my way to the Center as best I could. I am sure I dislodged a few books and I know I took a few bruises from the sharp corners of desks and clothes hangers. Irritated bankers looked briefly up from their screens, and I think I heard 'Look out, moron!' once or twice. But I got there.

Dark figures jostled for space at the entrance to the Global Center of Excellence. It wasn't a real entrance, just the place where a turret-like protuberance jutted out from the main building, creating a semidetached open workspace outside the main one. Badly lit because it sat in a kind of no man's land between two grids of strip lights, this transition space was obviously never meant to be such a hub of activity, the borderline between two very different populations who met in unceasing conflict and anger.

I felt hollow in my little blue silk suit from two seasons ago. I hoped my blouse, washed in soap since I had run out of detergent long ago, would stand up to the smell test. My mental pantyhose was unravelling.

A man in his forties was sitting just inside the Center, next to a huge pile of documents with differently coloured cover sheets. This, I thought, must be the notorious Front Desk where work was accepted from the bankers and re-distributed to the graphics people. The guy was kicking back in a swivel chair, eyeing everyone suspiciously. He wore a brown woolly jumper. Bankers pushed past me and kicked me in the shins. Didn't they notice?

I wrestled my virginal time sheet out of my bag and proffered it as far forward as my arm would reach.

'I'm Nyla', I said. And got no reaction.

A banker shoved me in the back and closer to the supervisor.

'I'm Nyla Nox', I repeated, 'it's my first night.'

The front desk guy looked at me, then turned round and said into the room: 'Another one of those newbies.' There were some appreciative giggles.

I continued to hold out my sheet.

The front desk guy, my supervisor for the night, swivelled back and took it. Unprepared, I held onto it for a moment too long and was left with a little piece of paper torn off between my fingers.

The front desk guy smiled. 'Sit down!' he said and turned towards the banker behind me.

Finally, the nervousness contained in my stomach had communicated itself to my emotions. I felt like the rabbit again, hopping up from the burrows of the Third Basement where it could hide to find itself in an open arena, surrounded by predators everywhere. The little rabbit made a stupid little joke.

'It's my first night', I said, 'please be gentle with me.'

As soon as the words were out of my mouth, the room behind the front desk fell silent. In spite of the apparent chaos my future colleagues were clearly able to pick up every word.

The supervisor didn't even look at me again.

I walked into the Center. Now I could relate a little to the visual secrecy – if people could see this, they would all want to live here. Visually speaking.

The room, it had to be said, was fabulous, or would have been if you could actually see it because it was stuffed to bursting with (much smaller) desks, documents, printers, assorted boxes and, of course, my future colleagues. I hadn't expected this but midnight was the busiest time at the Center. People were signing in and out, bankers wanted to go home or were struggling to meet their deadlines at 2AM or 4AM.

But when I raised my eyes I could see the famous long, narrow windows that really did run on all four sides, giving the Center the air of a small cathedral. Right now those windows were black with midnight but I was sure if you got close enough you could see the luminescent London nightline. The only side that had to make do with two smaller windows at the corner was left of the entrance as you came in. With their backs to the only solid wall, S&I were ensconced behind manuals and evaluation papers, overlooking the room from specially constructed elevated platforms. I automatically looked for our Trainer but he didn't do graveyards.

I gave one more glance to the night sky behind the windows and hoped for a beautiful view in the morning. I was too far away to see the stars.

To my anxious eyes, the room was full up. Desks were pushed close together, but instead of the L-shaped bankers' crosses in the Field of Desks outside, ours were short and narrow, lined up in crammed rows with workers on both sides. Half of us were facing the beautiful West Window, and the other half was left to face the entrance and S&I. Running down the middle of the rows were little half hearted cardboard divisions.

I thought all the seats were taken, but that was not true. There was one still open, right in the middle of row one, flanked by two operators looking away as I went to take it.

The seat and its monitor were in full and direct view of S&I. I turned and saw for the first time Lucy's face, framed in dark flowing hair, waiting for me.

Peter had not been lying when he said that S&I would be looking over our shoulders.

While I was trying to get my bearings and power up my computer, the woolly supervisor caught my eye.

'I like my newbies next to me', he said. 'Here, do take this job, will you, and hurry up a bit. They are waiting for it.'

He dumped some papers on my desk, chaotic, scrambled notes and sketches. Even as a novice I could see that it had no discernible style, nothing even remotely connected to the guidelines for the sacred Page that had been drilled into me down in the Third Basement. Even the company logo, memorized and retraced so many times, was different.

'How shall I –'I said.

No answer. He was gone.

Reflected in my monitor I could see Lucy's face, inscrutable, pale as moon light.

The pool of silence around me deepened.

I dug into my keyboard and tried to find the document on the system. Aggressive pop ups asked me to 'register!' I felt a hot flash of panic. Clearly there were many things we had never practiced in the Third Basement. Why? I had not time to think about it.

'Get on it! Get on it!' hissed the Front Desk. Ok, it really didn't want to start out looking like an idiot but it seemed I had no choice. I turned to S&I for help. Lucy was gone.

I didn't give up, not then. By trial and error I stumbled on the necessary procedures to let me log in. But it had cost me precious time.

And I still had no idea what to do with the strange looking document.

For a moment, helplessness overwhelmed me. It was like falling into a deep waterless well. I had been abandoned, thrown to the wolves. The job I had been given was impossible to do. Everyone was watching. Was this first night going to be my last?

The thought of money jolted me out of my paralysis at the bottom of the well. I simply could not afford to be fired. I had to stay here, and I had to survive here, whatever it took.

I spotted Lucy standing at a desk further into the room, and as I ran up to ask for her help I could hear her compare laptop prices with a very thin operator drinking peppermint tea. They both gave me outraged looks.

'I am talking to Des', Lucy said.

'But, I need your help…'

She turned her back to me. Des took another sip. I could feel people watching but when I looked they were focused on their screens.

I went back to my seat and tried again.

'Learn some manners,' said Lucy, suddenly standing over me.

I would have said yes to anything. She helped me locate the file on the system which I could never have done for myself, on that first night. Together, we looked at the page that wasn't a Page. With a little smile in the direction of the Front Desk, Lucy said 'I'm afraid I can't help you with this. That's not a style we do. You're on your own.'

Then, departing, 'bring it over to show it to me afterwards for corrections.'

Then the bankers came.

First came the youngest one, carrying all the papers.

He wore a new but slightly smelly suit and never told me his name.

'New markups', he said, throwing another stack on my desk, 'the traffic lights.'

I clicked through the document and yes, here they were. A row of circles in groups of three, one underneath the other.

Red, orange and green, garish and brutal, an insult to our sophisticated colour scheme.

'Buy. Hold. Sell.'

When I touched the first circle, it blew up and engulfed the whole screen. The banker instinctively took a step back. I wished I could do the same. In fact I wished I could just jump up and run away. Instead I tried to reduce the blob to its original size, then just to reduce it, to any size, as long as it was smaller, but it stayed a giant red.

The banker, hanging over my right shoulder, made an impatient sound.

In my panic I deleted the red blob altogether. At least that still worked.

The page came back but now one of the traffic lights lacked the bottom red.

There was 'Buy', there was 'Hold.' But no 'Sell'.

I reached for the next red circle. Maybe I could make a copy and replace the first one with it. I was just clicking on it, when the next two bankers arrived.

And produced another explosion.

The two new bankers pushed the first one aside without even looking at him. 'Moron', I heard one of them say.

And to me, in sharp staccato: 'Show me, show me, show

me the markups.'

Papers flew.

My red circle degenerated into a blood tinted oval, reflecting Lucy's stern face.

The bankers ordered me to close the file down. 'Now! Now!'

'We are going to have to start from scratch.'

I dimly remembered there was an emergency template, somewhere, for projects without a style (but wasn't that for experienced operators only? I seemed to remember the Trainer's voice, warning us not to try this on our own). I hunted for it on the system while the bankers were arguing with each other at the entrance. One of them seemed to have all the information, while another one seemed to have all the power. The third one was relegated to answering his phone in a panicked voice.

Desperately I tried to catch the shift leader's eye.

The shift leader kept his back turned. I turned around in my chair. 'Lucy! Please!'

A sigh. 'What is it now?'

'The red dot…'

'Oh', Lucy said, 'yes, that's a bug. It doesn't work.'

My fingers were ice cold and tears stood just behind my lids. I tried to tell myself not make such a big deal out of this but my body knew otherwise.

My fellow operators looked away and soaked up every word in silence.

The bankers returned.

'Let's leave that', the oldest banker said. 'It's no use.'

For a moment it occurred to me that the bankers had been stitched up in this too. I didn't know why but maybe they did.

Or maybe it was completely random, and we were just set against each other as an experiment, like animals in the Colosseum.

One thing was clear, and it was clear to me from that

night onwards: this was no way to maximise shareholder value.

'Someone needs to take charge here', said the oldest banker, who revealed himself as top-of-the-three. He leaned over me and gripped my mouse. I could feel the hairs on his hand brush against my skin. He tried to lasso a complex table and insert it. And failed miserably.

For the first time, he looked me in the eye.

'You are incompetent', he said. His voice was laced with the black ice of contempt. 'Incompetent'.

'Incompetent', echoed the second banker, while I tried to regain my mouse. This I did actually know how to do.

As I fixed it, the top-of-three banker walked up to the Front Desk.

'I want another operator!' he shouted.

'She's incompetent', said the second one.

The operator to my right who had been successfully invisible until now perked up and gave me an amused look.

The shift leader refused to budge.

'No', he said. 'I haven't got anyone else.'

A ripple of released tension went around the room. A line had been drawn in the sand.

'You'll just have to make do with her', the shift leader reiterated and swivelled a little in his chair.

Lucy's reflection smiled, or perhaps the monitor was distorted. Two operators further down the room resumed a quiet discussion of private school rates.

The operator to my left took out a pack of diet biscuits. She exchanged a glance with Lucy and asked the banker who was still standing next to me to give her a little more space.

He bunched further in, ramming my chair into the edge of the desk. My arm jerked all over my pad and I lost the picture I was carrying with my mouse.

I said nothing. Trying to conceal my shaking, hand on mouse, eyes on keyboard, I fixed the damage.

'Ok', said the top-of-three banker, returning from his

failed fight with the supervisor 'let's try again with what we've got.' Now he was projecting the air of a disaster recovery expert.

The second banker stalked off.

For the next two hours, the bankers and I were rotating in a poisoned circle, Sell, Hold, Buy. Looking back on it, I didn't actually do all that badly. I did manage to implement most of their requests, apart from the bugged red dot. But at that point, it didn't matter anymore. The bankers were convinced I was incompetent and their reaction was to shout at me and bunch me in until their day old suits rubbed the shoulders of my little blue silk jacket while tried to work.

They questioned every move I made. They ignored every mistake I fixed. They changed their minds all the time, and blamed me for trying to follow their conflicting instructions. Around 2AM they stopped talking to me altogether, just muttering sarcastically to each other how abysmal my performance was.

When 3AM came round, I began to feel they were right. My stomach had fossilised around my non-existent breakfast long ago.

You may think 'but it was only three hours', you may think 'why wasn't she stronger, why didn't she just disengage?', 'why didn't she stand up for herself?'

I simply couldn't.

I was in a hostile, unfamiliar environment where my financial survival was at stake. It was my first night in a new job, trying to use newly acquired skills. I was shouted at. I was out of my depth. I failed. I knew I was being assessed by people whose agenda was impossible to guess. And all this was happening in public, in front of a silent, but by no means inattentive group of my future peers.

It was also 3AM in the morning.

Any sense of proficiency that I had achieved by passing Basic Training down in the Third Basement was gone. I could feel it, my brain and hands became clumsy. I could hardly type any more. I felt worse than the crumbling pieces of a rat.

It was the mental and emotional equivalent of being beaten up for three hours in front of a crowd who did nothing but seemed to quietly enjoy the spectacle.

Looking back, it's a classic scenario. And it worked.

Somehow I managed to reconcile the document, layer the graphics and put in minimal company styles. The banker who had stalked off returned, carrying coffee only for himself. At 3.30AM a phone call came in to the youngest and the bankers were instructed to 'pull the plug'.

'Is it finished?' I asked in a quaky voice.

The first banker invaded my key board one last time and saved.

They left me in their dust.

Suddenly I really, really, needed the toilet.

'You're not going anywhere, Miss!' Lucy's voice caught me right between the shoulder blades. 'You come up here and show me your work.'

PTSD

I went home feeling small, dirty and useless.

The sun must have risen behind St Paul's but I did not see it.

I clung onto the slippery poles in the crowded bus at 8.30AM and tried not to fall. The night had gone on as it had begun. After 4AM, when I had finally finished Lucy's corrections, I was able to go to the toilet (and I now got an inkling of the significance of its location). The original bankers from the red-blob-no-style stitch-up were long gone, but I was set one near-impossible task after another, and I failed them all.

Although I was desperately tired, I couldn't sleep until well into the afternoon. And when I slept, 'incompetent' echoed through my dreams.

My stomach took another day to loosen up. Porridge at 9PM?

Later, much later, I was asked by a kindly counsellor if I had any symptoms of Post Traumatic Stress Disorder after working in this environment. If I did, if I do, I believe they hark back all the way to that first night. And all the nights that followed.

Survival of the Fittest – body and soul

Many years later, I sat on a tombstone and looked up the sheer, stark wall of the Building without a Name. What was really going on here? What name could I give to what was going on there, what was done to us inside its dirty, convoluted corridors?

I had a lot of theory to choose from, a lot of history to compare it to.

What it seemed to coalesce into, with the century old chill seeping into my tights, eyes blurry and mind whirring from exhaustion, was a deliberate Social Darwinist system, designed to brutalise junior members in an attempt to select what the Bank thought of as the 'Fittest' who would survive and rise up the ladder of evolution to conduct its business (and by implication, lead the world) one day.

I had been tired for a long long time. The gravestone was unrelenting. My friends were nowhere to be seen.

From that perspective, I could see no point in deceiving myself any more. What I saw, what I had become part of (although at a very very low level, so low that my position on the evolutionary ladder of survival was somewhere between 'scarcely out of the mud' and 'inferior prey') was a system that divided people between 'superior' 'natural leaders' who are the winners, and 'inferior' losers who deserve the treatment they get, at the bottom of the heap.

I could have made this analysis on my very first night. But I didn't.

In fact, it took me several years to arrive at this conclusion, partly because I was afraid of my own thoughts, but mostly because the system worked. I was attacked, beaten up, demeaned and publicly exposed as 'incompetent' in front of my superiors and my peers. On my first night, and for many nights to come. And although, I did not really feel inferior to the bankers on a general human level, and although, unlike them, I had read the philosophers, the historians and the anthropologists, the best that Western culture has to offer, somehow, deep inside, I became what they saw in me.

The first money

A few days later, I had money.

There it was, on the thin piece of paper dispensed by the ATM.

I stared at it, I blinked a few times. Tears were possible. Who would cry at the ATM? From now on, my wealth would no longer be measured by coins in a pocket. My next rent was safe. I could buy washing powder. I could start on my debts – at some point.

This was my reward.

I was back in civilization.

Bankers' bodies

Military metaphors came easily at the Most Successful Bank in the Universe. The Field of Desks with its many crosses that I traversed exactly six times per night resembled the Field of Honour certainly at least in one respect: over 95% of the bankers were men.

In the weekly emails we received from our CEO, he often congratulated himself on his diversity policies. And there was some truth in that, in terms of nationality and, up to a point, in terms of ethnic background. We had bankers, and operators, who spoke many different languages. Spanish, Russian, German, Italian, Chinese, Japanese, French, Arabic, and many more. (In terms of racial diversity we could point to a few black graphics operators and security guards but not many black bankers, at least not in London.)

The bankers worked in 'industry teams' and in so-called 'country teams' but they also, all of them, spoke excellent English. Although the Bank was an American bank and the location was in England, native English speakers were in the minority. Every night on the Seventh Floor you could hear a beautiful collection of the 'Englishes', the diverse and individual versions of English as a global language.

In spite of this great diversity in the Center and our ability to create Books in virtually all known tongues, the shift leaders were almost always British. This was of course not a written policy and it took me a while to notice it.

When I first joined, there were almost 40% women in the Center. Some of them had been there for some time, some even pre-dated the Center, having risen from other support functions. Some were hired along with me. But over time, our number declined steadily.

The bankers, on the other hand, were almost universally in possession of a penis. We saw a few females sometimes in the bottom rung intakes, and we all knew the two notorious ladies from different country teams on the second lowest tier. Female top bankers were rumoured to exist and occasionally appeared on TV. I always looked out for them but unfortunately, I personally never saw one.

The bankers had their own gym on the ground floor, and they worked out a lot. Lean muscle tissue was just as much a desired feature in a banker as in the bulls and pigs they ate. They spent many hours glued to their seats, storing up fear, boredom and anger, and then they went down to the gym to release them. Other times, they released them on us, and on each other.

As a result I was surrounded by young, well toned, testosterone filled men in a wide range of looks. It should have been a great place for the enjoyment of male beauty, a place to flirt and look out for favourites, or even have an affair.

The bankers themselves should have been happy to see us, the (increasingly elusive) women of the Center, but that was not so. Maybe it was because of their existence in the trenches, where every instinct was dulled except the one to survive another day, maybe it was the class differential they perceived between themselves and us (winners and losers, predators and prey in terms of the Bank's Social Darwinist system), maybe it was their monk like dedication to their work, maybe it was another reason altogether but there was never much action between us and them. Or, really, anywhere in Bankerland.

Once, a young banker started a survey among several hundred of his peers and found out that less than 1% of them currently had a girlfriend.

'I wouldn't bring a girl here', said one of the lucky few, looking at us and not seeing us, it seemed, 'not with all those hungry guys out there.'

Around this time we all received a mandatory email from Systems, telling us that any websites we visited could and would be traced to our individual sign-on ID. All of us were required to report any 'accidental' hits on pornographic websites immediately and with all necessary details, including how we got there.

Who am I? – My contract with the Bank

I am tempted to break out in song and insist, at the top of my voice (and slightly over the top of my register): 'I'm Jean Valjean.'

But unfortunately I was right at the other end of the process: my identity was about to be broken, not re-asserted.

When the agent sent me my contract I saw that I didn't have one, I had two.

My first contract was not with the Bank, but with the agency who 'supplied' me. It was never made quite clear to me beforehand that I would not be a direct employee of the Bank, but on a kind of permanent temporary assignment from the agency. But I also never asked directly, my mind was fixed on the money. Not that there would have been another option anyway...

It all became obvious when my first pay slip came in. The agency, with its headquarters in the beautiful Georgian town house just behind the Bank of England was my employer, in the eyes of the law and the inland revenue.

However, apart from the pay slips and the send-off to the Test, and from the two phone calls I received after the Test and the Training, I never heard from the agency for almost two years. And then only because of some very very unusual circumstances…

All my instructions and the entire framework of my job were determined by the Bank. That was my second, very long and detailed contract. I signed it to that effect, but again it took some time and experience to realise what it meant in practice.

It meant that I carried out the Bank's work as if I was their employee and had to obey my supervisors, my managers and their managers and so forth all the way up the line to the CEO in New York, but legally I was a casual worker provided by an agency who received none of the Bank benefits (except tea, coffee, sugar and real milk from a fridge) and could be fired overnight. Although, as I discovered, that last one could happen to real employees, too. Nobody was ever safe at the Most Successful Bank in the Universe, not even the CEO.

I was not allowed to seek any kind of alternative employment while working for the Bank, I had to preserve its secrets for at least two years after I left or was fired (but got no pay-off to compensate for that). I also had to sign a piece of paper declaring that I was not a member of a trade union. Organised labour was a firing offence.

We were then given another big book with all the company guidelines, including anti-discrimination and anti-harassment policies. Obviously, such a big book would have to be read in our free time. I still wonder, to this day, what the purpose of this big book was and who else, besides me, had ever read it…

Later in the graveyard with Peter

'Oh my first night', Peter said nonchalantly. It was nice to look forward to a chat with him in the morning after work when we shared a shift twice a week, Thursday and Friday.

The gravestones were cold on our bums but the air was fresh and free outside the nondescript door leading to the dark passage.

'Bad stuff. Ignored and despised.' He laughed and shifted on his part of the marble. 'Luckily I had Rita and we could talk together. Still, I know what you mean. They really try to bring you down.' A shadow passed over his face, perhaps thrown by one of the feral falcons seeking out its hunting ground. Then he gave me an engaging smile. He stirred his coffee. I pulled my jacket closer around my shoulders.

'Rita?' I said. 'You're friends?' I didn't like how that came out, a little sharp.

'I hardly noticed her before we came up on the shift', he said. 'But I'm really glad she's there with me. It makes a big difference, having a buddy. Down in the Third Basement I was more occupied working out a system with Ilya, cheating the training tests.'

'Oh that's what your bromance was all about?' I said.

'Yes', Peter answered, his smile broadening. 'Of course. It was actually his idea. We would swap parts of the assignments and do one half each.'

I remembered Julian and how the agent was 'on his case'. I remembered the guy whose name I never knew who disappeared within the week. I remembered the public announcement that I was 'not a visual person' (and my hot shame…). Meanwhile Peter and Ilya had their system…

'So what happened to you on your first night up?' Peter lowered his voice sympathetically.

'What's the name of that woolly guy? The shift leader?'

'Woolly - oh, Hank!' Peter exclaimed. 'You are funny.' He gave me a longer, deeper look.

'He threw me to the wolves', I said, 'They all pretended I didn't exist. They gave me a job that was impossible to do, working directly with bankers who said I was a moron…' I had to stop. I nearly cried. I didn't want to cry.

'I forget, of course', said Peter, more softly. 'You were alone.'

'Yes.' I didn't trust myself to say more than that.

Yes I was alone.

I wasn't quite sure, should I be ashamed for being alone? Or proud that I survived anyway?

'Not any more', Peter said. 'See you at midnight.'

Only when I was riding the bus home, it struck me that since my first night had been on a Thursday, Peter must have been there, too. Somewhere in the silent crowd.

Unless he was sick, of course. I never asked him.

Claire

I learned fast. Week three and I was still there. I was also well ahead with my survival kit: bags of food, easy to eat at the desk, complete with plastic spoons and sporks, sachets of lemon drinks against the flu. Food was necessary at the desk, because there was no break to eat it in, no break at all during our eight hour night shift.

I also needed a novel to read on the three buses that took me to work, and a big blue jumper against the terrible cold blasting the Center from its hyperactive air vents. It wasn't for nothing that the veterans called it 'Siberia'… Next week I would be able to afford an underground travel card which would cut my journey time in half. In theory, we were able to come in by minicab if our shifts started after 11PM, for safety reasons, but that, unlike the tea, coffee, sugar and real milk from a fridge, was a taxable benefit, which meant in reality that we were paying for most of the taxi fee ourselves. So safety was a luxury good.

I waited. Sign in was taking its time. I had arrived early, but the shift leader's signature on my sheet was what counted. Literally. I was paid by units of 15 minutes, and pay for the first unit could often be cut off by all sorts of measures and reasons, and so could the final unit in the morning, resulting in the loss of half an hours pay per shift. At the discretion of our shift leader. While management slept in their suburban homes, hours of train rides away.

I stood in the queue. My fingers hurt. The plastic bags with my survival kit were biting into them.

I still didn't know any of the colleagues who were ahead of me in the jostling queue, much less the bankers who completely ignored me except when I felt their elbows in my stomach. Nobody had introduced themselves to me, and I had not been included in any conversations. On the few occasions when I tried to contribute a remark, there was an icy pause, just a few seconds' worth of it, and then they just moved on as if I was not just invisible but also inaudible. Remarks by them about me, though, were frequent and very audible indeed. They mostly concerned my incompetence and lack of manners. So far the only ones who had acknowledged my existence were Peter (nicely) and Rita (grudgingly), S&I (critically), and the shift leaders (when necessary to maintain the chain of command). While engaged in our work, none of us were supposed to speak at all (although some trusted old timers did seem to enjoy that privilege through some as yet undisclosed process of merit and preferment) and we were reprimanded if we disobeyed.

My fingers were getting numb. Not good. I put my bags on the floor. Deep red ridges ran along my hands. My time sheet had suffered a little, too, being squashed alongside the shopping. I tried to smooth it out against my skirt.

The queue advanced. I was pushed from behind and kicked from the front.

My bags rolled over on the floor. One of them ripped open as I tried to pick it up. The guts spilled from its belly and onto the floor.

I bent down quickly, managed to push the orange in, and scrambled for the carrot pack, and the little piece of bread left over from yesterday. But where was the cottage cheese? Suddenly I felt such a craving for cottage cheese... Sleep deprivation plays havoc with your balance of emotions. And hormones. And regulation of appetites...

Ah, here. Interesting, the carpet only looked black when you were standing up. Up close it was greyish with sprinkles. The cottage cheese had fallen on its side, rolling away from my searching hand, but I grabbed it. It felt damp.

I pulled frantically on my bag.

Something blue and sharply pointed stopped me in my tracks.

A shoe.

'Sorry', I heard myself say.

The shoe advanced.

I retreated on my knees, dragging the bag with me. The cottage cheese was seeping white stuff from a central cavity.

The shoe nudged my fingers.

I looked up.

Into small, sharp features and very blonde sculpted hair.

'I'm Claire', she said. 'Your shift leader.'

Immediately, my brain kicked into gear. Forget the cottage cheese, this was mission critical. Claire… Wasn't she evenings? I must ask Ilya, he was in touch with rumour. What had happened to the woolly guy?

Claire didn't say anything further, just watched as I awkwardly stood up and extended my crumpled time sheet towards her. She held it up against the light, for all to see, exchanged a glance with pale faced Lucy from S&I, and signed it very slowly, daintily holding her pen so that her fingers wouldn't touch it. We both knew I couldn't get a new time sheet because the signatures from the previous nights would never be replaced.

'Sit ', she said, leaving me to hook the sheet under my little finger.

Then she turned round and gave a hearty greeting to one of her friends a few rows away. The friend, a chubby guy with a management manual slipped under his keyboard, politely enquired after her health.

'Well, Ethan', the shift leader said, 'funny you should ask. I still have this ache in my tummy and I was wondering…'

I didn't know then that I would listen to this conversation, and all its cousins, so many times that I consider myself qualified to give a detailed report on Claire's medical condition, all of her medical conditions, and there were many, this very minute.

Stumbling into the Center, I saw Peter stuck in the seat in front of S&I.

'News!' he mouthed at me.

Of course all the good seats had been taken.

There were only two left, one of them directly next to the

front desk. At least Peter had been able to avoid that one. The other one was in the middle row, facing away from the entrance.

Anything but the one next to Claire. Maybe there would be an opportunity to upgrade later on, when the 2 o'clocks went home.

Murmuring soft apologies, I dumped my things on the desk. My orange immediately rolled unto the adjacent workspace. The ruined plastic bag gaped at me. I knew how it felt. And the cottage cheese was now mixed with dirt from the carpet. I felt something akin to sorrow, completely inappropriate to the loss of a cottage cheese, but not uncommon at the start of a graveyard shift. I could see Rita sitting further down the row, still wearing one of her big men's shirts. How had she managed to circumvent the dress code? And how had she managed to snag one of the better seats facing the entrance? She avoided eye contact.

I sat down and switched the terminal on. Of course the cut off time to be entitled to the first 15 minutes of pay had passed, although the 15 minutes themselves had not.

'Your jacket is hanging over my desk', said the guy next to me. I recognized him my first night, Lucy's peppermint tea drinking laptop adviser.

Before I could say or do anything, my orange rolled back to me. And my neighbour was executing a painstaking wipe down of the border area adjoining my desk space. Used wipes stacked up next to my left hand, scrupulously marking the dividing line. Cleaning fluid scented the air. I half expected Rita to snigger but she didn't. Something had silenced her up here, in a very short time.

Eight hours on the graveyard with no breaks

Before I worked at the Most Successful Bank in the Universe, it never occurred to me that there might be jobs with no breaks. Not now, not in Europe in the 21st century!

Even when we were Training down in the Third Basement, we had regular breaks every two hours or so 'to absorb the knowledge' (and for the Trainer to keep up with developments on the Seventh Floor).

And we complained those breaks were too short!

Now, on the Seventh Floor, and for all the time I was there, we worked eight hours with no breaks at all.

Again, this was not in the contract, nor was it ever mentioned by the agency.

When I came up on the Seventh Floor, I didn't know.

On that terrible first night, I just bounced from command to command, from disaster to disaster. I worked when told and ran to the toilet when I got the opportunity. I thought the morning would never come and then, suddenly, it was light and another day.

The next night, working my way through a less stressful job, I sat and observed. As far as I could tell, nobody took a break, so I didn't either. The third night I tried to go to the toilet at 1AM.

Immediately, the supervisor rocked up in front of my seat.

'You don't get up every hour', he said. 'Oh no, you don't'.

'Sorry.' I sat down again on my full bladder.

'It's not our culture', said Lucy from her perch. And indeed, it was not. In the Center of Global Excellence, when we worked, we worked. Breaks, obviously, were for other, weaker people at other, weaker banks.

'And put in your eye breaks, or I can't sign your sheet.'

What were 'eye breaks'? No one responded to my query.

I got the details from Rita and Peter, whispered across the desks when our leaders were otherwise occupied, maybe with a banker complaint, maybe with holiday snaps.

It turned out that, every night, we had three five minute breaks, which must be taken at least two hours apart, spaced out over the shift, and lodged in our time sheets. These breaks were a legal requirement for people who stared at their screens non-stop, such as data entry operators, and we were actually on shaky ground here, as the supervisors sometimes reminded us, since. we also spent a lot of time looking at documents (and considerable time looking at Claire and members of S&I). But the Bank, in its generosity, had decided to give us the benefit of the doubt and paid us for those 15 minutes break per shift . 'One whole unit for free', said the supervisor and cut my final 15 minutes of the night because I had finished my job a little early. The eye breaks could be denied or postponed for business reasons. But usually, we got them. All three.

The traitor in our midst!

'Don't you know', said Ilya a few nights later, taking his sweet old time to vacate the seat I coveted, right under the West Window, and that I had raced to claim against fierce competition and at the price of dirty looks all over the room, 'Hank was fired.'

'No', I said. 'I didn't know. Was it on the company emails?'

Ilya halted proceedings completely to give me a pitying smile.

'No, of course not', he said. 'There is no email when people disappear. They're just not there anymore. You have to figure it out.'

'Ok', I said, certain that I never would. From now on and forever, or until the banks closed down, I would have to rely on Ilya's intelligence gathering services.

'In fact,' Ilya continued, finally manoeuvring the style bible into his bag, 'he was escorted from the premises. By security.'

'What?'

'He had to pack up his personal stuff while the guards stood over him. They took his pass and they marched him out, just carrying a cardboard box.'

Ilya motioned me closer. Claire was fighting with a bunch of bankers, so we were safe.

'He was suspected of passing on information to competitors', he whispered.

I could hardly believe it. The woolly guy! He seemed the last person to have all this criminal energy.

'Well', continued Ilya, 'we know a lot of secrets, after all.'

We did?

So far, I had not noticed the content of my Pages much. I

had told myself that this was because I wouldn't let my mind be contaminated by too much commerce but now I wondered. Was this the reason why nobody explained anything to us? So that we couldn't betray them?

'Yes', said Ilya. 'of course. More secrets than the bankers ever will.'

'I'll take your word for it', I said. 'Can I sit down now? I have a 1AM deadline.'

Can you get me a mortgage?

'So now that you work at the Bank', said my friend from outside (outside? Since when was I 'inside'?), 'can you get my parents a second mortgage? For my next house?'

'Well', I said, trying to wake up at the dinner table in the nice restaurant (my friend was inviting), 'there's a short answer and a long answer.'

'You see', said my friend, 'now that I've come back from the dig in Peru, and going out to the China survey next month, I'd really like to buy a house. We're getting a little past the age of renting, don't you think? We need to grow up.'

She shook her glossy chocolate brown hair which she was letting grow out again after the rigours of her South American expedition. I resolved to die rather than reveal the truth about my bedsit to her. So I nodded at the hair story, hoping she would just accept it as a general nod.

My friend returned the general nod with an equally general smile.

'My parents have it all locked up in their own house but now's the time. Can't go wrong with real estate.' She smiled again, taking my nod graciously for granted.

The cocktails came. They were beautifully presented with flowers in creative glasses. I cautiously sipped at mine. The taste and the alcohol made my eyes swim. But in a good way. 'This is lovely, thank you', I said.

My friend took a deep gulp of hers. 'So?'

She looked at me with a mixture of hope and entitlement. She was still working in anthropology. She had bought some of my old books.

I realized that, unlike most people, she would probably not have a mortgage of her own either. Just like me, only completely different.

'The short answer is No.'

My friend put her glass down and looked hurt.

'The long answer is this: the Bank doesn't deal with customers like you.'

'Why? I have an excellent credit rating.'

'Or me.'

My friend looked doubtful.

'But if I just walked in there...'

'First, you would never find it. Second, it's not that kind of bank.'

'There are different kinds?'

I tried not to sigh. Not so long ago, I had been just as innocent.

'The Bank has no individual customers. Only companies. It doesn't give loans. It certainly won't give your parents a mortgage.'

My friend looked puzzled.

'But then – it's not a bank. Is it?'

'It's an investment bank.'

My friend started to chew, but she was not convinced.

'But what does it do?'

After that dinner, and of course after my graveyard shift, I came home in the morning and looked at my depleted row of books. I took out the old reports from my project. I had LOVED being an anthropologist. If someone had offered me a project right then and there, I would have left everything behind and joined up.

Except of course that I needed money...

I cried until lunch time.

I wanted to hit my friend with her glossy chocolate hair but it wasn't her fault.

'Actually', said Peter when I told him the story, 'what you

told your friend is not entirely true. The Bank does have private customers.'

'Really?'

I couldn't help looking around. Where?

Peter smiled.

'You're still thinking like someone from outside. The bank only deals with private customers who are as rich as corporations.'

'People as rich as corporations...' I tried to imagine what their lives must be like but my imagination deserted me, looking out over the Field of Desks.

But Peter was right. In fact, he showed me the door, down a quiet cul-de-sac. 'Private Wealth Management.' Whoever the customers were, we never saw them on the graveyard.

2AM

At 2AM I was working on a job that was estimated for an hour 'or so' but the 'or so' did not appear on the cover sheet. The all-important Estimates were made by the Front Desk when the job came in and in theory depended on the length and difficulty of the job. In practice, they depended on mood of the shift leader.

By now I had understood that I must show each piece of work to S&I and afterwards do their corrections, even if the job had been closed down. Again, nobody ever told me this but I learned by trial and error, by reprimand and failure.

'Until you pass your three months' assessment.'

Here was another piece of information that had not been given out in advance. In spite of all the Tests and Trainings, this was the hurdle that really counted. For the next three months, I was not really part of the team. I was a probationer.

Right now I worked on my 'one hour' job, afraid not to finish it on time and afraid of the moment when I finished it.

Somewhere in my field of vision I could see Rita rummage around aimlessly on her desk. She stacked and re-stacked her papers and tidied her mouse pad a few times before finally getting up. She took her print outs and the marked up pages, then pushed her chair in and out several times before she started walking. Something was slowing her steps.

Peter, opposite her, shot her an encouraging look, just a few seconds too late.

Lucy's pale face lit up as she watched Rita's slow progress down the rows.

Claire pushed her bag out a bit so that Rita had to stop and acrobatically step around it without losing her stack of papers. Behind her back, Claire looked at her chubby friend Ethan. Ethan looked back.

And then Rita stood before Lucy's desk, humbly awaiting notice. Lucy's dark hair streamed down, hiding her face.

The Center fell silent. Des the laptop expert took a sip of peppermint tea.

This could take a minute, or four, or more. Lucy was a master of suspense.

When she finally looked up, Rita would have to hand her printouts up to the S&I fortress. Then, she would have to wait again while Lucy corrected them.

Still Rita stood with her back to the room. Something looked strange about her shape - oh yes, she was now wearing a skirt under her oversized men's shirt and over her leggings. The skirt looked old and disused. I didn't feel I was the frumpy one anymore, but it brought me no pleasure. On the contrary, I was shocked. What had happened to her up here?

The silence grew more intense. I could hear Des swallow his tea.

Without lifting her head, Lucy held out her hand. Rita gave her the sheets. Lucy's hand stayed up.

'Thank you', Rita said.

A sigh went through the Center. Lucy's hand went down. I could hear her shuffle the sheets. We returned to our own jobs, but every time we looked up we could see Rita standing there, in front of the raised platform, awaiting her judgement.

In spite of the Siberian air condition, I could hear Lucy's pen scratch the paper. It was a red pen, of course, and it left heavy indentations, sometimes ripping the material apart. I had seen often enough what it could do on my own faulty efforts. I thought I could distinguish the special sound that made a circle around a mistake. Something in the wristwork…

Finally Lucy was done. She started to read out her corrections, a long long list. Loud enough for everyone to hear. It was painful. And it was also distracting me from my own work, ensuring that I would have plenty of mistakes in my own pages, when the time came. Rita listened. And then she was told to step up and 'look at it'.

Claire crept closer to Ethan for a better angle. Ethan moved his management manual away.

There was only space to balance on one foot on the narrow ledge of the elevated S&I platform, and that was what Rita had to do. In that position, and looking at her heavily redlined work, Rita had to repeat Lucy's critique, sentence by sentence, aloud, and publicly admit to her mistakes. She was then sent back to her seat to do her corrections.

Rita looked at no one on her walk of shame. She pulled her chair out and sat. We were able to focus on our work, at least for now. Peter pushed a tissue through the partition.

'What do you think, Lucy', said Claire with the air of a reasonable person pursuing an academic debate, 'Ethan and I have been wondering if their work should be checked a second time after they've been corrected. I mean there's no guarantee that they'll do it right, is there, if we don't control them.'

Des nodded eagerly and raised his peppermint cup. I noticed again how skinny he was, almost as thin as Claire. Maybe they were both suffering from the same stomach ailment.

Although it had been a little distracting to work with all this going on around me, my one hour job was now done. I saved it one last time and went to printout. I was next.

I kept my mind fixed on the three months' assessment…

Why didn't Rita leave?

I didn't really like Rita.

Down in the Third Basement, I had thought she was rude and nasty. But now I wanted to see her feisty old self back. Instead, I saw an adult forced to wear clothes she clearly disliked so that she could work in a place that showed her no respect.

Rita was an artist, very focused on herself. Too focused on herself, I had thought. Why then didn't she stand up to them, why didn't she refuse to change, why, if all else failed, didn't she leave?

At the time, I never asked myself this question. It just never occurred to me. We all wanted to stay, for as long as the Bank would let us, and the more difficult it was to survive there, the more we clung to it. Also, by this time, we all had money coming in, regularly, every week. If I kept my mind fixed on the money, maybe so did Rita. Maybe I had been right from the start, and Rita was poor too.

Angry bankers

But where were the bankers?
Well, of course, they were all around us.
From the moment we came in, we could hear them. Loud and clear. Their main method of elocution was shouting, a sound that, magnified by several hundred on a working floor, resembled constant gunfire, both distant and alarmingly close.
We saw them at the Front Desk, where they slammed their papers down on the surface, demanded first class treatment, threatened to get everyone fired, and seemed to be absurdly vulnerable to slights and disruptions, real or imagined. If I hadn't known that drugs were absolutely prohibited on the work floors, I would have suspected them of smoking something...

But the bankers' brand of paranoia needed no chemical assistance. And after watching them at close quarters for almost two months, I started to make a few guesses as to why that would be.

Junior bankers, while trying to convince themselves (if nobody else) that they were big dicks because they were in 'high finance', and destined to be one of those 'natural leaders' the Bank constantly preached about, were in reality at the beck and call of their superiors every day, and every night, and had to jump to their every whim. Like us, but much more intensely, they were also obviously going through a 'rigorous' selection process of the Fittest. Most of them would stay at the Bank for two years or less, and only a tiny percentage would make it to the top, where the action was. And, of course, the big money. But, unlike us who were being groomed to accept our dismal fate, the bankers were kept alert and alarmed through a constant rollercoaster of hope and disappointment. Anyone, they believed, could make it to the top, if they had what it took. While of course in reality practically no one could make it. Just numerically speaking. For people who had been trained in statistics at the best universities in the world, they were remarkably gullible.

Banks were later criticised for doing business in the way of a casino. Perhaps this was not so surprising since the internal business of the Bank had long been a lottery.

The bankers often looked to me like packs of dogs, never able to establish a lasting hierarchy, biting and barking all night and (presumably) all day, because they all knew that they had to prove that they had what the Bank prized the most: the elusive, admired, and ill-defined quality of 'natural leadership'.

Yes, I could understand their anger. But…

The three months' assessment

If you failed it, you would not return to the Bank. Immediate termination.

If you passed it, you would no longer have to endure the nightly public humiliations by S&I, and you would be given, at least in theory, more interesting jobs. But the best thing about passing the assessment was that you would be allowed to listen to your own music on your own earphone while you worked. I had begun to crave music to an almost alarming degree. I fantasized about it while I listened to the aircon, the supervisors, the raging bankers and the ritual corrections by S&I. I expected the music to help me retain a sense of my own self.

But even music privileges were not unlimited in the Center of Global Excellence, as Claire reminded us several times per night; operators who had passed their assessment were allowed to put in one earphone, one earphone only per head, so that they could listen to the shift leaders' instructions at all times. Looking around me I saw a number of old timers with one earphone in and the other dangling down over their desk. To me it looked like a badge of distinction, proudly worn. Some old timers comfortably complained about the unreliable radio reception.

Claire herself never listened to music. Earplugs would likely have ruined her rigid hair sculpt but mainly she preferred to talk. She talked almost non-stop, a continuous eight hour monologue that only went on pause when S&I pronounced their judgements on the newbies. If she didn't have any bankers or if she wasn't handing out instructions she gave long lectures on the correct way to behave or perform tasks, unwritten rules not mentioned anywhere, all of them, and all of them absolute law on the graveyard shift. The fate of past offenders was darkly alluded to. Some of these people had had to have long talks with the invisible managers in the daytime. Some of them had been reported to the agency. And some of them – well, some of them were no longer with us.

Claire's voice penetrated into the furthest chambers of my awareness.

In our small crowded space it was not possible to avoid the waves of stress, pain and fear that spread out from her. It was exhausting.

But not as exhausting as my fear of failing the assessment. Although I now enjoyed the power of detergent on my blouses, I had not even started on my debt repayment programme…

The Bank's only tangible product

… was produced in the Center. I began to understand that this was why we were so important. And why there was so much pressure.

'The proof is in the pudding' was a favourite phrase of certain bankers. And if it was, the Center was the place where the pudding was whisked together, and cooked, and decorated with a mint leaf.

The Bank's clients paid vast sums of money for its advice, but all they ever got to hold in their hands were the Books (brochures, booklets and pitch material) we produced. Our Books had to look as expensive, clever and comprehensive as possible to illustrate not only the project and the Bank's invaluable advice, but also the fact that such a large team had worked on it day and night, for weeks or months. Or sometimes even longer.

All the rest was talk, and meetings, and air. And over soon.

Indiana Jane

Coming home on the night bus, I wondered how I would describe our little tribe in a research paper. If I was still researching. Or to my peers, if I still had them.

Then I quickly thought of something else. It was too painful. My former peers were still out there, following their passion. While I had ended up on the graveyard shift.

Still, as I drifted into sleep, I could not help wondering who we were, how we could be described?

We somehow didn't fit any model.

If we were an extended family, dynastic tales could be told down the centuries. If we were a jungle tribe, real anthropologists, the kind I now never would be again, could visit us. If we went extinct, our customs could be reconstructed in a museum, illustrated by artefacts. If we were steel workers, or prisoners of war, we would have our own, defiant traditions. Michael Moore could make a gritty documentary about us.

Maybe this was a new constellation of the human tribe altogether. Maybe I could be the one to discover it… And then…

Old dreams are the walking dead.

Dream on Indiana Jane.

Here tonight, gone any moment

Every week we found in our inbox an email from 'Tom' from New York. Tom was the CEO of the entire Bank, and he was very optimistic about the future. All of us were contributing to it and we were the best and brightest. (Tom did not distinguish in his messages between real employees and disposables like us – he included everyone in his forward thinking.)

Every night I scanned the room for unexplained absences. I knew most people on the shift by sight now although many still kept communication to an absolute minimum.

'I can sense a black hole the moment I'm signed in', said Peter.

Absence could mean holidays, special training or sickness, but also 'sudden company death'. It could mean that the colleague had been fired that morning.

Ilya said they never gave a reason. Or a warning.

It occurred to me that the only other situation where survival was this uncertain would be an army in war time.

Every night could be our last.

The eye break

'I'm going for my eye break', I said. Claire let me pass then shouted into my back.

'Five minutes means five minutes!' I nodded out of habit

although she couldn't see it. Nodding when Claire said something had become a learned reflex.

I was taking the five minute 'eye' break I was entitled to every two hours.

I had already taken my first eye break at 2.30AM to race to the toilet. Now, two hours later, I still hadn't decided whether I really needed to go again or whether I could afford to visit the kitchen, make myself a coffee and take my yoghurt out of the fridge.

At 4.30AM the field of desks was mostly deserted. So were the outer offices running along the windows on all four sides. Rumour had it that the glass walls of those outer offices were the result of a very public sexual harassment law suit that some bankers from the Trading Floor of the Bank had lost a few years ago. As was its wont, the Bank angrily over-reacted and those transparent walls were the result. I imagined the aggressive ripping out of the previous office walls, the Bank venting its anger with hundreds of saws and hammers, furious executives coming to listen to the violent slashing and to stare at the jagged edges of shattered card board.

As I squeezed my way past the hard wooden edges of the desks (still no path for human bodies here), I spotted a late gaggle of bankers at the other end. They would probably turn up at the Center soon. Many of the desk dividers had towels hanging over them, drying in the night air and absorbing whatever it carried into the crust of old sweat from endless morning gyms. The desks themselves were actually hard to see, so overloaded were they with newspapers, partly cannibalised pitch books created by the Center, memos, regulations, taxi numbers and take out menus.

A little further on I ran into the sharp end of a clothes hanger. It carried two jackets and another one behind it carried a freshly laundered shirt, still in its plastic sheet. If you were a banker, you could get all your laundry done and delivered to your desk, something that often came to my mind when I dragged my dirty washing to the local launderette. I could see the kitchen door now and realised how much I wanted a stimulant. My mind and mouth were in coffee land and so I didn't see the feet sticking out from under the final cross until I almost tripped over them. Almost. Something stopped me at the last moment, maybe a shadow on the floor, the primitive survival reflex of mammals acquired on the steppes of the stone age.

Whatever it was I was glad it had stopped me. Right in front of me lay two feet in black socks, twitching slightly, and attached to black trouser legs curled up on the floor. I had always thought this was just a company legend but no. I had just found my first banker sleeping under his desk. He had taken off his jacket which hung from yet another hanger and for a pillow he had rolled up another towel. He was cuddling his mobile phone in his hand.

I knew it meant wasting another fraction of a minute but I stepped softly around him. I didn't want to disturb his sleep. In my mind I saw long dead soldiers, not much older than him, sleeping in the trenches, their heads on their provision bags, holding their rifles close for comfort.

Cannon fodder.

The kitchen

But while we were still alive, we had a kitchen. It was tiny and served several hundred people, night and day.

I raced to the kettle and put it on. Luckily there was still water in it and it was even a little warm. Less time to boil. For the second, third, fourth time. Who cared. It could only make it safer, I told myself. I tried to use my time efficiently by simultaneously searching for spoons but couldn't find one. I told myself it was ok while I shook clumped up instant coffee directly from the container into the styrofoam cup, also a tax free benefit although Claire felt there was a limit to what people should be able to scrounge. Why not bring in your own mug? Since we didn't have permanent desks, we would have had to carry them back and forth with us on the bus, with the rest of our provisions.

Our kitchen on the Seventh Floor had two fridges. One was full of milk bottles, except at the weekend when they ran out. Right now it still had a reasonable supply of blue, red and green caps. A few nights ago I had seen Des screwing off the tops of all of them until he found one that was still untouched, its silver skin unbroken.

'The bankers drink directly from the bottles, I've seen them', he said. He never used a bottle more than once.

Some of the bottles I was looking at now had been probably been opened by Des. Others had the saliva of bankers' mouths dripping from their rims. I chose one at random – life is a lottery.

The second fridge was the food fridge.

I decided to retrieve my yoghurt, even if it would take me the rest of my allotted five minutes. I tried to remember all the identifying details: it was cute and small, and it had pictures of cheerful chubby cherries on it.

Boldly, I opened the door. Several boxes fell out. One of them hit my foot. It leaked a brown liquid but the frozen core still packed a substantial punch.

When we came in at midnight, the food fridge was so full that you had to jam your food in anywhere you could. Other people would then, in their eye breaks, take your food out and if you were lucky jam it in again in some other place where, if you were extremely lucky, you could find it again. If you were unlucky, it got lost. If you were very unlucky, it would be left out to rot.

The kettle boiled. I stuffed the half thawed boxes back into the fridge and made my coffee. My yogurt was consigned to the annals of time. Maybe the sweets machine. Later. In my next eye break at 6AM.

On my way back with the coffee I saw Peter, navigating the desks a few rows over. He waved at me and crossed to halfway distance. Rita, still in what looked like the same skirt I had seen her in last week, didn't follow.

'Pity you didn't tell me you were going on your break', he said. 'We could have had a chat.'

I nodded. I would have liked that. But it was too late now. I could only take his smile back in with me.

Claire was looking at her watch as I passed the front desk. She always wore a watch and looked at it, in addition to the big clock on the Center wall and the cosmically accurate one on our system.

'Six!'

I promised to make my next eye break shorter to compensate for the extra minute I had taken. Claire only snorted. She knew the operators would always take advantage – I had heard her tell Des and Lucy many times. Ethan was always ready with examples.

As I sat down I regretted that I hadn't chosen a trip to the toilet instead. But that would now have to wait until after 6AM. Until then, the coffee would keep me awake.

And a message full of coded smiles from Peter.

What I bought with the money

A big breakfast. That was one of the first things. I went to a nice café, I bought the newspaper, I spread it out on my table and ordered. The money I spent could have kept me in home made sandwiches for a week but I didn't care. My breakfast covered the entire table, and there was tea with it, made in a pot, and orange juice with pieces. I finished it all.

Clothes took a bit longer, and so did shoes.

But now that I had washing powder I could stretch my existing clothes a long way. When I needed warm tights and new underwear for inclement weather, I was actually able to buy them.

And then I went on my first day trip on the train down to Brighton. I sat on the pier and watched the sea gulls. I had my chips stolen by them. I pushed pennies into the machines. I walked and breathed and everything smelled fresh and alive.

Did it happen?

Ilya looked pale and exhausted because he was studying full time while working the evening shift at the Center.

'Well you have to', he said. 'You can't stay here.'

Peter agreed.

'Yes', he said. 'I'm studying too. It's the only way. I'm going to have a better life.'

By chance we had both arrived early and were already

signed in, waiting for desks.

'What are you studying?' I said.

'Well, you know I have a degree in philosophy', he said.

I did.

'Now, I've decided I'm going to study something useful for a change.' Peter looked at me defiantly. I knew he felt loyal to his first choice, a nice trait in a guy, really. But if he had decided to join the other side, well, I could see his point. I could see it all around me.

A gaggle of bankers jostled us on their way to the kitchen. They always took right of way, whether they had it or not.

'Let's go downstairs', said Peter. 'Just for a moment.' He turned and almost touched my hand.

It felt deliciously daring. 'Alright.'

I knew that some of the bankers who smoked went downstairs in the middle of the night, standing in the rain and the mist rising from the gutters.

Waiting for the elevators, a delightful tension rose between us. Why hadn't I seen this earlier? It could have thrown a nice pink veil over the harshness in Siberia.

'Well, tell me what it is then', I said.

'No, no. Wait.' He smiled but didn't touch me.

So I didn't either, which was lucky because at that precise point, Ethan came out of the elevator door and shot us a hard glance with those sharp blue eyes of his.

Peter kept his word. He wouldn't say until we had gone all the way down. We walked boldly out of the main entrance into Shoe Lane, past the bankers' black cabs running the meter on company time and then round the corner into tiny Cobblemaker's Row.

'So?' I said. 'Is it a secret?'

'Not really', said Peter. 'But it was nice to get you alone.'

This was quite possibly the most light hearted and lightheaded moment since I entered the Bank.

'We are alone', I said. 'So –'

'I'm studying computer programming', he said. 'I'm doing a course where you can learn it in one year.'

'Really?'

'Yes. In a year's time I'll be off earning four or five times what we make here. And it will be a good job. Something that uses my intelligence.'

Now it was my turn to smile.

'Will you call me when you are rich?' I said. 'I could be your –'

'You could be that now', he said.

There was no one about in Cobblemaker's Row, if you didn't count the dozen homeless sleeping in the doorways.

'Yes I could', I said.

He kissed me.

Then we had to run to make the cutoff point. Even another kiss was not worth the trouble. That night, I felt so warm inside that I never felt the cold wind blowing down my neck. Of course I didn't let on in the Center. That would have been flirting with danger. And talking about flirting…

Instead I relived the moment.

In the morning we got separated. The next night was a Saturday and Peter was off.

Had it really happened?

The big swinging dicks

'Ah', said my friend from the outside, another friend this time.

He looked at me with envy and resentful admiration.

'I know. Investment bankers. Traders. Champagne. High class call girls. Fast cars. Thousand dollar tips. Bing swinging dicks. Right?

Glamour.

You'll be stinking rich now.'

I thought of our kitchen and said nothing.

Tom's teams

After the rush of coming in, of making the cut-off point for our time sheets, after fighting for a desk and getting our first allocated jobs (Boring but safe? Interesting but much more painful when the time came for public reprimand? I wouldn't have known what to choose, but then of course the choice was never mine anyway), every night, around 1AM, we entered a special danger zone. It was called 'working directly with the banker'. This was the fate worse than death that everyone tried to avoid. But of course not everyone could.

Oh, the eyes of the shift supervisor scanning the room, looking for someone who could be pulled out and sacrificed. In an instant, those who had considered themselves lucky by being given an all-nighter straight off were now at the short end of the stick. It was truly a lesson in impermanence.

Claire didn't like having bankers inside the Center, and kept them away as much as she could. After midnight, she had a lot of power and she used it. However, with an urgent deadline and a project signed off by a senior guy, she had to cave in. But someone would have to suffer...

I knew all the danger signs. Tonight, she asked loudly for a volunteer. Sometimes, very occasionally, some kindly soul would raise their hand. Maybe they would again tonight. I was never one of them. On the contrary, I lied about my deadline whenever I thought I could get away with it so that I wouldn't be pulled out. Maybe those saintly volunteers really liked it, I would tell myself. Maybe they enjoyed the buzz and the direct involvement... Maybe they were earning points for paradise.

Most of the time the shift supervisors couldn't remember who they had given which job to. They started to walk the rows and demanded to see the deadlines on the front sheets of our jobs (this was when lying about them got tricky). Various tactics were employed to hop off the devil's shovel – some people never looked up, some volunteered for a tea round, sacrificing 15 minutes pay, some tried bold and outright falsehoods (only the more experienced ones), but that invariably led to ugly complications later on.

Always, always one of us was chosen.

Then the banker, who had been standing at the Front Desk all this time, watching our lack of enthusiasm and the fearful selection process, would be asked to go and 'sit with that person over there'. Names were not divulged. Fair enough, I never knew the bankers' names either.

Oh no. Oh no. Tonight, it was me. As humans always will, I tried to second guess fate. Was it a coincidence or was there meaning behind it? If so, what was it?

'My' banker (as soon as Claire passed him on to me, he was 'mine' and remained so until I was able to get rid of him) bounded up to the West Window, seething with rage, and leaned over me.

From his point of view, I (as part of the Center) had already wasted his time. From my point of view I was now sure that I had been maliciously dipped in it (again), and I sincerely wished he would trip over my neighbour's chair (this particular neighbour always stuck his chair out quite a long way because he assumed the kind of working position that you would on a recumbent bike) and break his nose. Both of these feelings were entirely understandable. Seething both, we started our collaboration.

'Our Bank has consistently shown that it is better than the others. We succeed in good times and bad', said Tom's most recent email. 'This is because of our culture of teamwork. People are our capital.'

The banker snapped out his instructions, very fast to make up for lost time, and barraged me with a lot references to other parts of his project. I tried to follow, but couldn't distil the information I needed. He didn't understand why. For the last six weeks he had spent all his waking hours working exclusively on this project, and so had almost everyone else he had seen in that time.

'Please', I said when he drew a breath, 'I don't know anything about this. Please, I'm starting from zero.' Everything I said was closely monitored. By Claire, over at the Front Desk, with her super acute hearing. And by her special retinue of oldtimers. Out of the corners of my eyes I could see internal messages, called 'webflashes', blinking on their screens. Quite possibly I wasn't supposed to see this, but then, also quite possibly, I was. It could be a warning to me. It could be a warning to others.

The banker muttered something under his breath. I felt lucky it wasn't out loud.

'Please', I said, 'I want to help you. Just tell me what to do first.' The banker looked at me with disdain. His idea of my intelligence level had been confirmed. Well, so be it, if it gave me a chance to do his job. I really didn't want him to call his pack.

I was fighting on two fronts. On the one hand, I had to satisfy the banker's demands. On the other hand, I had to follow and if necessary enforce the company style guidelines to satisfy my supervisor, S&I and ultimately the invisible managers.

As so often, this was the 257th markup of a Book that had been copied from a 'legacy' project in a different industry in the first place. Markups were often in the hundreds, and often contradictory in nature. If they could have stopped calling me a moron for five minutes, I could have felt sorry for the bankers who had to reconcile all these conflicting demands from their superiors and who, just like me, saw a reasonably well designed product being butchered mercilessly and pointlessly. They knew just as well as I did that this markup was not the last, even if the deadline was near, and that, however well they did their job, most of it would be murdered on the altar of seniority. The markups also had a tendency to introduce mistakes – I knew this mostly because I tried to spot as many as possible so I wouldn't be blamed. Bankers had the luxury to vacillate between fury and fatalism.

As usual, 'my' banker had tried to cram content to fill five pages onto one, largely the result of accommodating everyone's markups and avoiding to give offence. This however was dangerous for me because it directly contravened our style guidelines. Like Napoleon, I was losing on both of the fronts I was forced to fight.

The bankers were always, always angry. Their anger was

passed on to us from their own superiors, and the way they themselves were treated, but the underlying cause was the terrible shock to their life-long self-image – little princes reduced to cannon fodder.

Just to get here, to the Most Successful Bank in the Universe, they had been selected and selected again from an early age as part of a super-elite, the best and brightest, exceptional young men who went with ease from one extremely competitive achievement to the next. Leaders of the future, destined to be the masters of the universe. Their idea of themselves as truly and innately special had been confirmed many times, and not only by their mothers.

And now they were cannon fodder, ready to be culled. They had only a short time to make their mark while at the same time preventing hundreds of competitors, sitting right next to them in the field of desks, from making theirs. And as if that was not enough, many of them who had believed they were the rightful champions in an unbiased meritocracy were faced, for the first time, with the harsh truth that the brutal randomness of luck would play a big role in their fate.

I overheard them complaining that they had been unfairly allocated to the losing teams, or to winning teams where they were forever unfairly overshadowed, and certainly to the teams where others were taking all the credit and they themselves were doing all the work. Never mind what they had studied at Harvard, credit taking and blame shifting were quickly turning out to be the most vital survival skills here and, apart from luck and perhaps a rare chance to impress somebody higher up who could act as a godfather, credit taking and blame shifting would seal their fate. Unless of course they were VIPs already by birth (and announced as such in the company emails) and so were in a sense their own godfathers. Nothing could touch them then.

Nobody on the outside knew the real facts of what went on and who did what in the project teams. It was all a matter of make-belief organised by the select few. Everyone else was at their mercy. And nobody seemed to want to know either – the Bank showed zero interest in promoting the best.

Leadership was based on a different kind of merit, something that many bankers realised far too late. In a way, those little princes in all their arrogance and disdain for what they regarded as inferior life forms (such as me), were very very naïve.

The higher someone rose in the Bank, the less access they had to reality. Information was highly doctored and distorted by the time it reached them. What they were presented with was just as much a work of fiction as the shift reports from Claire to those managers we never met.

It may seem strange that the bankers, and the manager bankers, and the very executive bankers on top of them all (including Tom) would not wish to know what actually went on in their own company. Surely, information was power? Not so. Reality was irrelevant in this as well as in most aspects of investment banking. The tales that replaced it had a powerful magic. The Bank had its narrative, its myth of heroes and losers, and doing the work well had very little to do with it.

On this particular night, I spotted, in an obscure corner of a secondary Page, the name of a company that had nothing to do with the industry this book was aimed at.

'Oh', said the banker, 'that's from – must be from the original template.'

'Shall I take it out?'

'Of course!' he shouted again. There was no daylight between shame and anger.

I took the offending company name out. The banker tried to breathe deeply.

'All we do is copy', he muttered under his breath. 'I wonder what we studied for at Harvard. Might as well work in the Center.'

There was also no daylight between his shame and mine.

I closed my eyes for a moment, wishing I could invent shutters for my ears. And then I could stop working altogether...

The banker was both stuffed and right – 'copy and mutilate' was the system at Most Successful Bank in the

Universe. Although, what did we know, mudcrawlers both of us? Quite possibly the Pages that were copied again and again were already so excellent that they could not be improved upon.

Data for the Bank Books were gathered by the junior bankers like my young friend here who copied (sometimes correctly, frequently not) information and figures for those Books from the internet, public sources and our clients' own material. In fact, using the material the clients themselves had supplied was so popular with the junior bankers that we regularly received IB wide emails urging them to stop doing this, because the clients had noticed, complained about, and started to question the added value of the Bank's analysis and advice. They had just been sold back their own product!

The clients of the Most Successful Bank in the Universe did expect and were promised 'customized' or even 'tailor made' solutions for what they proudly regarded as their own precious and unique situations. After all, the Bank was supposed to know things nobody else did and could penetrate the darkness of economic confusion as well as predict the future. I have no idea how much our clients knew about our processing methods but in reality they were part of a 'one size fits all' production line. One company was like another. Just like sheep are like one another. Except to other sheep, of course. They all make wool.

Nobody, but nobody in investment banking would possibly have tolerated being called a sheep. Wild dogs and predators to a man.

After all my time at the Bank, reading so many of their Books, I am at a complete loss to understand why the clients kept coming back, and kept paying our exorbitant fees for a service

('copy and mutilate') that was insultingly incompetent and had been discredited time after time. The only explanation I can come up with is that they must have been true believers in the natural leadership of high finance, and as such impervious to evidence.

I am at an even greater loss to understand why the Bank

itself wasted so much time and effort on such an inferior product that failed to live up to its own description. After all, we were not one of those inept public service bureaucracies where the staff got sick leave and pensions.

And far from being blasé about it, I find the whole thing alarming in the extreme, considering that very far reaching economic and political decisions were made based on the Bank's advice and analysis, decisions that affect us all.

I never once heard a banker express any concern whatsoever about this monumental internal waste of resources and routine deception of customers.

One thing though became clearer and clearer to me: whatever the purpose of all our work here was, we were definitely not maximising shareholder value. Almost as if we didn't need to...

It was only much much later, when I realised what kind of world I was living in, and when I also realised that I was absolutely capable of understanding it in spite of all the myths to the contrary, that I took the simple step of informing myself where the profit of the Most Successful Bank in the Universe went: almost half of it was 'compensation' of its top executives. The natural leaders who climbed the ladder to the top. Who were running the Bank for their own personal profit.

I would never buy their shares.

In spite of the fact that the teams were so vast, and so much of the work was either very simple or copied from somewhere else, or perhaps because of that, the bankers were always under terminal time pressure. The version of the project that I was working on with 'my' banker of the night would have to be finished, approved and processed in production (good luck boys!) by 3AM. The bankers fuelled all this by anger, fear and contempt. And, rumour had it, in spite of all official precautions including sniffer dogs at reception (but only on the day shift) by other substances, although they never shared them with the Center.

'Did you hear how that banker fell off his chair?' said Ilya.
'No.'

'Right in the middle of the Sixth Floor. One moment he was sitting at his desk, doing his thing, the next moment he cramped, he clutched at his chest, he spilled his coffee all over himself. And then he just dropped. Dragged a heap of papers after him. Rolled about a bit. Then unconscious on the floor.'

I looked at Ilya, not knowing what to say. Could this be true?

'He must have come in here quite a few times', Ilya continued. 'But I can't say that I remember him. Anyway, I hear it was towards the end of a long project, on and on, you know. Coffee, shouting and no sleep. Apparently he had been saying, only a few months to go, only a few weeks to go, only a few days... and then he dropped.'

'Did he have a heart attack? A stroke?'

'They never found out.'

Meanwhile, 'my' banker was getting angrier. He managed to infect not just himself and me but everyone around us with his destructive mood, another reason why 'working with the banker' was so unpopular. He must have so much surplus energy, I thought, or maybe that was how he kept it up. Maybe if he whispered he would fall asleep.

One thing that worked in my favour was that the banker had nowhere to sit unless he was willing to carry in a chair and push it between me and my desk neighbour – and some bankers were perfectly capable of doing that. But tonight I was lucky, and 'my' banker's fashionable shoes were clearly killing him as he leaned over me. I could tell because he had started standing on one foot, then shuffling over to the other.

As soon as he would let me get a word in, I tried to encourage him to leave so that I could get on with it. After all, since he was going to have to get the job approved and fight with production later on, now would be the perfect time to go and have a break, a cup of tea, a bathroom visit, a look at his schedule, call his mother, log into a porn site, spy on his sleeping colleagues, anything, really...

What a relief when I succeeded and he went, threatening to call every ten minutes. I took a deep breath and did a few arm exercises over my head. Some of my desk neighbours smiled discreetly.

A little peace now, I thought.

'Have you finished then', said Claire. As usual I hadn't seen her coming.

'Not quite', I said. 'It's going to take another hour or so.'

Industriously, I put my hand on my mouse and kept my eyes on the screen.

'Ok, you', said Claire. 'Mind you hurry up. They need it for 3AM.'

3AM was written in huge letters across the pink front sheet on my desk.

Several answers crossed my mind that would have brought great relief to my feelings. For about two seconds, before they brought ruin to weeks ahead. So I swallowed them down into my stomach where they clumped up together with the unspoken retorts of the last few weeks. I could feel the fossils forming.

'Look at me when I'm talking to you', shouted Claire.

I couldn't help it, my head shot round.

'Yes, of course', I said. My voice was perfectly calm. Acid shot up my oesophagus.

I did it for the money.

'And then, show it all to Lucy', she continued. 'It won't matter to the banker, but it matters to S&I.'

The truth that dare not speak its name

Many times I thought I almost understood what was going on here, and then it escaped me again.

Of course I had no time (and no courage) to think on the graveyard shift, but when I was out in the day…

I lay on my bed in the afternoon, I opened a book from my diminished shelves. All the great thinkers were at my arms' reach, or could be googled in an instant. The values and ethics of two thousand years of Western culture were stored inside my head.

And yet, when it came to naming the truth, I fell into a mind fog every time.

Maybe it was the notorious dumbing effect of large group psychology. Maybe it was the differential between theory and experience. Maybe it was because the Bank's belief system usually went, even amongst its critics, under the more palatable name of 'Social Darwinism'.

But mostly, I think, it was because of the visuals. What happened here at the Bank didn't look at all like the way I expected this phenomenon to look.

And then, of course, because it was such a terrible thought in itself.

But slowly the pieces of the puzzle were coming together, and I could no longer pretend that I didn't recognize what I saw. And once I did, I realised that the difference between the Bank and the spectre whose outlines frightened me so much, was largely cosmetic.

It was true, the Bank was a very multinational (although perhaps not very multicultural) institution. The bankers came from all sorts of different ethnic backgrounds.

The bankers didn't look like the iconic Hollywood villains of a regime that had been vanquished decades ago in a war to end all wars (sort of…) and whose defeat was still celebrated constantly on all US media, so that I could be forgiven for thinking that we had forever left it behind on the scrapheap of history. There were no jackboots and grainy footage of screaming men in moustaches.

Yes that was all true.

But what I came, reluctantly, to recognize, was that the Bank's 'Survival of the Fittest' was perhaps just a new, updated version of that seemingly long eradicated ideology, and the reason why it had taken me so long to put my finger on it was that this new version had been de-coupled from the model of racial superiority.

Instead, race had been replaced by the concept of 'natural leadership'. Replaced by the idea of a small number of 'natural' supermen of any ethnic background (but clearly mostly of the same gender) who revealed themselves through the rigorous selection procedures of the Bank.

What I hadn't understood was that this concept of 'natural leadership' was really the concept of genetic superiority in a new form, the idea of an elite that was born to rule (although the exact genetic elements of this superiority were never made quite clear), while the rest of us were born to submit.

Call it what you will, but I reluctantly came to call it by its real name.

And I shivered under my covers, because I had never in my life called anyone the F word before...

The Bank, our Bank, the Most Successful Bank in the Universe, believed in and ruthlessly executed what could only be called a proto-fascist ideology.

Over the top

But when I went back to the Seventh Floor, everyone looked so normal.

There were no uniforms, no tanks, no mono-coloured shirts all across the workfloor, no emblems to rally to (well, perhaps apart from the company logo but a company needs to have a brand).

The young bankers were hostile and full of themselves, yes, but they were also just exhausted boys.

Tom had written us a nice letter, full of appreciation and encouragement.

And Claire was finally on a one week holiday...

How could I call all these ordinary people, how could I call the modern bank that employed us and provided finance for the world, the F-word?

No one else did.

The Center of Lost Humanities

One of my colleagues was a dancer. Another one was a clinical psychologist. In fact, the Center was full of artists, historians and philosophers. The kind of people who are often quoted as proof of human superiority over the animal kingdom. Throw a brick and you'd hit a PhD.

The majority of Center operators were at least as highly educated as the bankers. The difference was that the bankers had studied 'Business Administration' and then they went out and worked in their chosen field, living their dream in a career at the Most Successful Bank in the Universe. Those of us who had studied the 'humanities' went out and worked in the Center of Global Excellence, living a nightmare. Two opposing populations who saw each other as proof of everything that was wrong with the world.

But while everyone knew of the existence of bankers (without necessarily knowing much else about them), our own existence was virtually unknown outside the Bank.

Perhaps because it didn't fit in with any known parameters, perhaps because holding all this contrary concepts together in one place just gave them a headache, or perhaps for some other reason that I never discovered, outside people never seemed to understand what I did.

'Oh', my friends would say, 'you are working in a call centre.'

'Well', they would say, 'it's not unusual for creative women to end up in the typing pool. It happens, you know. But why at night? I don't get that', looking at me with disapproval, as if I was concealing the kind of night time job that is usually conducted in the back streets of King's Cross. (I often passed my fellow night workers there on my way home when I was short-shifted at 5AM.)

After a while I stopped explaining. Something was going on here, something that prevented people from hearing or from remembering what I told them.

Was it possible that people (well, actually, my very own friends) were taking a certain amount of satisfaction in the idea that someone who used to be like themselves, an intellectual with big dreams, or maybe just a friend, a member of their imaginary peer group, had failed?

Failed and was drowning in the typing pool...

Graveyard remix

'Hi Peter!' He was ahead of me, a quick morning slalom between the headstones, holding his briefcase in one hand and his travel card already out in the other.

'Peter!' He heard my voice and slipped on the wet grass. I felt bad but it was a chance to catch up. Which I did.

'Hi Nyla', he said, steadying himself against the rough stone. He still held the travel card between his fingers.

'Sorry', I said. 'Didn't mean to startle you'.

'Sorry', he said, too. He looked into my eyes. His were large and brown and I wanted to throw my arms around him. Instead I leant against another headstone and tried to appear cool and distant.

'I'd love to stay and talk', Peter said. 'But I'm already late for my lecture...'

'Oh.' So much for being cool. I felt foolish. I didn't have a lecture to go to. Or anything else except bed.

'Let's go have coffee some other morning', he said. 'I'd love to.'

He was declining an invitation I hadn't even made. It sounded very smooth and practised. Was Peter a girl magnet? I hadn't thought so but if I liked him...

'Yes, let's see when there's a good time', I said. I started to walk towards the road.

Peter nodded.

When he lifted his hand I could see that he had grazed his skin on the gravestone. Tiny red marks shot up underneath but were not quite bleeding. He would carry that all day. To remember me?

He saw what I was looking at.

'Not the worst thing that's ever happened in a graveyard', he said, meeting my eyes and laughing a bit.

'Whoo hoo…', we both chanted at the same time. More laughter. Everything can be funny after a night shift, and when you're not quite sure if you're flirting or if you should be. Or if it's all nothing anyway.

Short shifting

At first, when I heard I had the weekend shifts, I was delighted. They were the best paid shifts of all. Like a milk maid, I started counting unearned money.

But what I didn't take into account was yet another important aspect of our contract that nobody had told us about – and this one packed a lot of punch.

(Again, I must ask the reader to suspend their powers of disbelief. I certainly had to suspend mine, but I had the evidence of nightly experience, and of my bank account.)

Who wants to spend their Saturday night at the Bank?

Well, a lot of bankers did, obviously. Therefore, we were needed, too. I didn't mind so much – I've always been puzzled by the idea that Saturday night is somehow more important than others. I can go out and enjoy myself any time (and while I was working on the night shift I also had a lot of interesting dates and meetups in the late hours of morning…)

The Saturday graveyard was a much smaller shift, and the atmosphere was declared to be 'very informal' and 'fun'. I didn't really find that, since we had some of the most difficult colleagues (of course, it WAS the best paid shift after all) on board and we also still managed to have Claire as our supervisor, on a kind of permanent (and well paid) extra shift arrangement.

But certainly the small Saturday graveyards made everything more personal. Oh yes.

First off, there was a lot of talking. The shift was mainly staffed by those who were allowed to speak on weekdays, too. The only difference was that, apart from me, they were now amongst themselves. Maybe they had been amongst themselves for a long line of Saturdays, and they didn't like the fact that I was suddenly there. I don't know who gave me this shift, but I wasn't going to give it up. I needed it. Particularly because of that other issue…

Coco, one of the old timers with entitlements, was engaged in an everlasting struggle with her weight and kept us informed about all the details of her failed diets. Right now she was 'totally dejected' but she might try something in the future, something that really worked, maybe from California where everyone was slim. Coco couldn't even look at pictures of herself and now refused to be photographed until she had reached her target weight (luckily she was safe in the Global Center of Excellence because of the confidentiality rules). She was disgusted with herself. And anyone was free to shoot her if they found her in front of the Sweets Machine. Really. Although they would have to bring the gun themselves and get it past security or kill her with a plastic knife from the communal kitchen… This brought on bursts of wild hilarity from Claire and Des who entertained the Saturday graveyards with mimicked stabbings demonstrating the bendable nature of those knives in more and more challenging conditions. I learned to be very careful and duck when, inevitably, the splinters flew everywhere.

Ethan didn't want to discuss slimming. He, too, had the fuller figure common among long term night workers and had long since decided to focus on his career instead. He therefore tried to turn the conversation to real estate. The others fell on it. Claire and Coco 'owned' houses in some of the nicer suburbs. They must be servicing heroic mortgages. Ok, Claire was a shift leader but Coco? Did she really earn that much more than I did? How far was she from paying off the interest? Ethan lived further out, half way to the coast, where debts slightly diminished but commutes stretched forever. I heard his travel card alone was 3,000 pounds a year. Des advised 'buy to rent' as the smart solution because there was clearly no way to get rid of those illegal immigrants so why not benefit from them? Claire reminded us again of her former boyfriend cum lodger and how difficult it had been to get rid of him, because the bastard had rights.

'Typical renter', she said. There was general agreement, and silence from me. They would never find out, unless someone betrayed me. But who? Not even Peter knew my dark secret.

'Do you remember Alessandro', said Claire.

'Oh, yes', said Ethan. He drank up and looked round at me, pointedly. I pretended not to see him. This was another feature of my Saturday. I had to make successive rounds of tea, was repeatedly sent back to the kitchen because I was useless and put in the wrong kind of milk which Des claimed he could taste 'blind', and was then forced to put another official unpaid unit of 15 minutes as a 'break' into my time sheet.

'Because otherwise it would be cheating, wouldn't it', said Claire sternly, checking her emails.

'He was always hiding at the back', said Des. 'And he never met his Estimates.'

They laughed.

'I don't know what he was doing back there, but it wasn't work.' This was even funnier.

'Well he's got all his time to himself now', said Ethan.

I sat there and longed for earphone privileges. The others all had their earphones proudly displayed on their desks, even if they were not using them.

As I turned the pages of my project, the discussion moved on to allergies and all the treatments that my co-workers needed. They were in constant agony.

It wasn't really a conversation in the sense that one person speaks and the others listen, then taking up the thread in response. It was more like one of those modern pieces, several independent streams of consciousness, clustered around loud harsh laughter.

Around 3.30AM I ran into a bigger problem.

My current project was coming to an end. I shot furtive glances to other desks. Hard to see how much they'd got left, because, as I had learned, there were so many different methods of stacking paper.

But I had already seen two of my more senior colleagues

exchange their jobs for new ones. Not good.

My speed was being monitored. I couldn't take the risk of taking too long or I might become another Alessandro.

So I walked up to the front desk, slowly, and tried to attract Claire's attention without offending her.

'Hi', I said. I sounded stupid.

'I've finished my job', I added, hoping I had judged the volume of my voice correctly.

Claire let me stand there for a while, then looked up.

'Alright put it over there.' Claire nodded to Des. Lately, Des had been given a lot of work to check up on, 'informally', on the Saturday graveyard. What was the significance of this? Could it be that Des, the blind taster of teas, was being groomed for higher things?

I took the opportunity to sneak a look at the pile of new jobs. There wasn't much.

'So', I said. 'So, now, what should I do next?'

Claire turned round on the swivel chair and leafed through the meagre stack of projects. Her blonde hair was a perfect, smooth surface. How often did she go to the hairdresser?

One job after another went into the 'not for you' heap. It appeared that, tonight, all the jobs that were left needed some special skill or training that I didn't have. But that, inevitably, at least one of my colleagues possessed.

One after another, the projects fell to the side.

I tried to guess the nature of those jobs from the colour on their front page. Yellow were the high end graphics, the ones I wouldn't be allowed to touch for another year or so. Pink I could have, in principle. They were the basic jobs, the ones that I could do (under supervision of course) but even there it wasn't all plain sailing. The fact that I was pink and the job was pink didn't necessarily mean it was for me. Some things were beyond the understanding of an ordinary operator like myself who hadn't even passed her three months' assessment yet.

But the shift leader knew.

I didn't dare look into her eyes.

'I'm afraid there's nothing here for you.'

I just stood there. Not again, I thought. This had happened to me every Saturday night since I first joined the shift.

'So I'm going to have to ask you to sign out for 4AM.' Then, generously, 'you can look at your best practices until then.' 'And call your taxi.'

Claire turned away. I could see she was researching buy to rent options in her part of London.

I kept standing there. I just didn't want to believe it.

Des and Ethan were watching me. Coco was watching them.

I could hear the air condition, not that that was very difficult. I could always hear the air condition in here, blowing and blowing its Siberian tune.

Claire turned and looked at me again.

'Anything else?'

Nothing to be done. I gave up and went away. Claire had absolute power over me on the graveyard shift, and she alone decided how much money I would take home that week.

This was my third month working at the Bank and I had never earned a full week's wages yet. My contract said I was only paid for the time I actually worked. No work, no pay. What it didn't say, at least not directly, was that I would be sent home at the shift leader's discretion, the moment the workflow dried up.

This practice was called 'short-shifting' and it overshadowed our lives every single night. It kept us in a constant state of fear and uncertainty.

Being sent home at 4AM meant I lost four hours' pay, half the money for that night. Considering that I worked four shifts per week, this represented 12.5% of my income. Other nights, of course, were also not safe from this practice although it was more common to be sent home a little later, usually around 6AM. The short shifting was unpredictable, and all throughout my years at the Bank, my payslip looked different every week. Strangely, this re-enforced our collective determination to stay in the job. Maybe this week I would be lucky, maybe this week I'd win…

The shift leader, of course, stayed every night, right until the end of her shift and sometimes beyond, earning extra time.

I wondered what percentage of its daily profit the Bank was saving by sending me home without pay. Did it really struggle so much to survive that it couldn't afford giving me a full night's wages?

The last thing I saw as I left was Des correcting my work.

I walked through the empty Field of Desks, and out through the glass doors.

My taxi driver didn't speak English and didn't know London. He tried to get me to sign for a longer journey than the one I took. I refused. He murmured a curse in a foreign language but I understood him. Only too well.

At the end of the week the money for the taxi ride was subtracted from my wages.

Not even the birds were singing yet. I thought of the people on my shift, still there, still earning money. They could spend it on whatever they liked, their mortgages, their cars, their dogs, their allergies. What about me?

After all, remember, I did this for the money.

Risks

My costs were fixed.

My rent, my water, my travel card. The only part of my expenses that I could reduce if necessary were my food and my phone bill. (I still hadn't started on my debt repayments.)

I worked for the same company, in the same location, in the same job every week. But my income was always uncertain. My pay depended on the volume of work we had each night. And that volume fluctuated wildly.

I had no influence over the Bank's workflow. And I had a

contract that prohibited me from working anywhere else to make up the difference. And anyway where would I find alternative employment at 4AM on a Sunday morning?

The Bank took the risks, and I paid for them.

Names from the past

Short shifted at 5.30AM. First train runs at 6.

I could pay for a taxi, or I could save my unearned money and wait in the graveyard. Why not? The sun is up. The dead don't mind. The rabbits run.

With half an hour to fill, I wandered around the graveyard. Not very big, occupying less square footage than the Center on the Seventh Floor. The Field of Desks could have swallowed it up many times over. And I have to say that the dead were even more cramped up than we were upstairs. Hadn't I heard that some of them doubled and tripled up underneath the cold old slabs that were the colour of decomposing bones?

I tried to read the names on the head stones, and sideways on the coffin shaped slate rectangles that served as seats while we ate our sandwiches. Most of the inscriptions were worn away by time, rain and pollution. But I could decipher a word here or there.

'Thomas', 'Anne', 'born', 'spinster', 'RIP'. One or two were almost complete, like 'John Ambersand, died of the plague' (year illegible).

Died of the plague.

Still rotting inside the earth just underneath my feet.

I wondered what his life was like.

Was he afraid?

Disclaimer

'This Page', the Trainer had said, down in the Third Basement before I came up to the Seventh Floor, 'is a disgrace.'

I prepared myself for the worst (something I wasn't very good at yet), but he was not making an example out of any of us, he was actually pointing to a Page that was included in every document.

Page Two in every one of the Books that were eventually compiled out of all our Pages.

'This Page was not set up properly', said the Trainer, 'and it is in All Caps.'

A gasp went through the class. Even then we knew that this was the Graphics equivalent of farting in church.

'But how come that this Page is in every book?' asked Peter.

'Ah', said the Trainer darkly, and suddenly we realised that even the power of S&I had limits, 'it was set up by the Legal Department.'

This page, Page Two, was the infamous Disclaimer.

We didn't work on Page Two. Nobody was allowed to touch it, except to insert the name of the client company in three specific spots. Any other alteration, however minute, could compromise the Bank's legal position, affect its financial viability and conceivably crash Wall Street.

So what gave it this awesome power?

Page Two basically stated, in no uncertain terms, that the document it headed, and all its contents, paid for by the client, did not under any circumstances constitute any form of advice and that the Bank could and would never, in all eternity, take any responsibility whatsoever for anything it had written in the Book, not even for the simple veracity of its data.

As I tried to delicately insert the client name, taking care that its Incs and Ltds did not interrupt the blasphemous chain of the legal All Caps, I couldn't help wondering what kind of business the Bank was in, and why its clients would pay so much money for advice (because that was what it was, in reality, however much it was Disclaimed on Page Two) that the Bank openly stated might well be wrong, misleading or completely meaningless.

What kind of advice was that?

Production

I had done my job, I had listened to S&I, I had made my corrections.

Now I was ready for the out tray.

'Stop!'

Claire, never the quiet paper whisperer type, had lately developed a habit of screaming as soon as someone's back was turned.

It worked every time.

I was jolted, Des chuckled, Ethan enjoyed himself more discreetly.

'You have to deliver this one to Production! The banker has left. They know.'

I sincerely hoped so.

At the end of the entire process, of setting up the templates, copying the information from other books and replacing it with (hopefully accurate) fresh data, at the end of the hundreds of cycles of updates and dozens of final versions, at the end of the ultimate reconciliation of figures and consistency checks for the right sequence of company colours, right at the end of it all, came Production.

This was when the Book would be printed and bound, in many copies, ready to reach its final destination. Production was extremely important for the polished and professional look with which we would impress the Bank's clients. But because of its position in the chain, right at the end of all things, there was never enough time for Production to do its work, or at least do it properly.

Therefore, visits tended to be fraught with tension and interactions between Production and the rest of the universe were often quite rough.

Still, my legs welcomed the brief walk through the Field of Desks, through the glass doors and out to the other side. Blood hesitantly started to climb up the veins, massaged and encouraged by the movement of my muscles. I flexed my knees and did a few balancing exercises in the lift. That must have been a bit of fun for security…

'Hi, Lenny', I said, trying to sound cheerful.

Lenny looked at me suspiciously from under the special cap he wore at all times. Production prided itself on the rugged individuality of its all male staff. Their blue collar credentials were underpinned by the huge machines and the deafening noise behind them. These machines must have been dangerous, because nobody else was ever allowed behind the counter, except on one memorable occasion.

Lenny, in reality a university graduate like all of them, took the Pages and looked at me sharply.

'5AM? You must be joking.'

'Well', I said. I couldn't remember ever joking in Lenny's presence.

'Not possible.' Now I knew why the banker had gone home.

We locked eyes for a moment, then I demurred.

'Sorry', I said. 'Can I call Claire?'

And 'Sorry' again when I got through to her.

Somehow it was probably my fault.

Graveyard remix

Could this be coincidence?

Again, Peter was just a short way ahead of me when I came out of the door in the morning. Briefcase and travel card in hand. How come I hadn't seen him in the small dark corridor?

'Hey, Peter!' I almost missed him.

This time he stopped straightaway. 'Nyla.' He said it before he looked. He knew my voice.

Suddenly, the morning seemed glorious even before my coffee.

Peter turned, without slipping this time.

He walked the few steps towards me.

'We'll have a drink, one of these mornings. Soon I promise.'

Did he think I was chasing him?

Was I?

'Alright', I said. 'Some morning, then. No rush.'

I tried to smile nonchalantly.

He smiled back with huge warmth. I could see most of his teeth.

Then he switched his travel card into the briefcase hand and stepped even closer. My nose rubbed against his jacket. I could smell a whiff of cologne. He must have refreshed himself in the men's toilet upstairs. He never wore cologne for the graveyard.

I smiled again although it was a bit wasted – Peter couldn't see it. He was tenderly touching my hair, lifting a few strands and winding them round his index finger, then tracing the line of my cheek and chin all the way down to my neckline. For a moment, he stopped there, then softly moved his fingers up again and tucked the strand of hair behind my ear.

'Really soon', he said, then turned away.

By the time I could think up a reply, he waved already from a distance, lifting his briefcase high above the headstones, and was gone.

I missed him so much it felt like a hole in my stomach.

Could people howl in the graveyard at 8AM?

I did not.

Instead, I consoled myself with a printout from the ATM.

My three months' assessment

...was overdue.

I knew it, I had marked the date on the calendar. Like a pregnancy checkup.

Why was it late?

It must mean something. Did it mean anything?

Peter hadn't had his either, at least as far as I knew. Neither had Ilya. But they didn't seem to worry. Of course, they had their computer studies, this was just a stop gap for them. On the other hand, didn't they need even more money than I did to cover their course fees?

What was going on?

'Oh', said Ilya, 'haven't you heard? It's the cull. They're waiting until after.'

Hot jobs in a cold climate

So I waited and worried in the summer heat, sweating into my bed while the sun never set before my alarm went off. ATM printouts rested on my pillow.

London can be very hot in summer, once it stops raining, and inverted weather layers trap the polluted air underneath. Going to work in the late evening, I wore a sleeveless summer dress, just like the people around me coming home from the pubs or garden restaurants. The underground was very hot, dragon breath in the tunnels. Even walking up the road to the Bank the air was mild, if a little smelly. Warm air transports olfactory particles more efficiently, and tonight's bulletin was that men were urinating everywhere. Against the walls of pubs, against the walls of underground stations, against the walls of graveyards and of banks. Summer nights were one great yellow liquid fest. I had become quite good at judging the speed of urine at various gradients, and also depending on whether the ground was tiled, in which case the flow was channelled along the edges, or smoothly surfaced in which case it tended to spread out. I learnt to stay well away from those in the actual act of urinating because their flow was unpredictable (and also because I didn't want to see them).

Usually I was successful and made it to the Center, a little steamed up dumpling in my summer dress and largely unstained sandals.

For the first hour or so I was warm.

But then I adjusted to the room temperature...

Around 2AM the cold kicked in, and it got colder and colder as the night went on. Sitting still in a chair for eight hours lowers your body temperature quite a lot, and then the bankers went home, each taking with him the several hundred watts a living human body releases into the surrounding atmosphere. Sometimes I drank cup after cup of tea just to get some warmth inside. I couldn't wrap my fingers around the cup, as you do in Antarctica and Scottish castles, because my fingers were needed for work. I couldn't wear furry house shoes because they just wouldn't fit into my backpack.

My impression on the very first day that the Bank was somehow a space ship was not altogether wrong. It certainly had its own climate, self-contained and separate from the city and island it was anchored in.

The air we breathed entered the building through huge filters on the roof. These filters had been there for many years, according to the work men who were very occasionally spotted on the day shift. The air was then pumped through the building inside many pipes, some of them intact, some of them broken, and all of them near-impossible to access.

Those pipes were home to a unique ecosystem of tiny and slightly less tiny creatures. Generations upon generations of them lived and died in there. Sometimes a big wind blew through the air conditioning and blew them away into another part of the building, and onto desks and hair and carpets. And cups of tea.

The fittest survived to form a new, improved colony.

Bacteria, fungi and assorted particles had adapted in a heroic Darwinian effort.

Waiting for the cull

People whispered. I didn't know what they were saying.

The bankers furiously produced Pages.

'They're going to be culled, too', said Ethan. 'So they need output.'

Claire embarked on an impromptu lecture about the annual cull. Every year, she said, the Bank fired a certain percentage of its people. From all departments. This included the bankers, the secretaries, the maintenance staff and – she paused until she had every eye on her, and every ear phone pulled out – of course it also included the Center. (Another way in which we were treated like real employees…)

She, Claire, had survived many culls in the past. Oh,

many, more than she could count. (one, two, three, four?)..

I noticed that not too many people were discussing their mortgages that night. Suddenly, the shadow of their debts loomed over their heads, mighty mountains that would come crashing down the second they lost their jobs.

'Last in, first out', said Peter, 'that's most likely.' Rita and I shuddered. Peter bravely faced facts, especially now that he was all set on his course and advancing. His ticket out of here, and into a better land.

'But when?' I said.

Not even Claire and Ethan knew.

The C word

Imagine the Savannah.

Bush land. Umbrella thorn trees, thigh high grass.

In the bright sunlight, a herd of elephants is grazing. Senior mothers and aunties stake out their claims, juvenile males test their tusks and several tiny babies weave in and out of their family's big legs. Everyone meanders purposefully, and the trees in their wake show evidence of it. The wildlife park is overgrazed.

Look up! A helicopter hovers over the land, over the elephants. Suddenly, it sweeps down. The herd, disturbed by the noise, turns towards their matriarch for guidance. She nervously twitches her giant ears. The heli comes closer. Dust swirls up. Elephants raise their trunks, loudly trumpeting their distress. The matriarch swerves from side to side. Babies hunker close to their mothers. A young male tries to charge the flying machine.

From the helicopter, the muzzle of a rifle protrudes. Shots ring out over the Savannah. The elephants can't hide. But they can run. All at once, following their matriarch whose superb memory has mapped out the best route out of trouble, inherited through the generations.

Unfortunately she is up against far more cunning minds now. Helicopter and gun drive the elephants in the direction of a bleak clearing surrounded by very tall umbrella trees. There is only one way in, and the elephants hope to defend themselves there. But when they arrive, two more helis rise from behind the trees. The first blocks the exit.

Deadly gunfire blasts everything that moves. Elephants scream in terror, then in grief, trying to save their babies. When they are all down, one of the helicopters lands inside the clearing and armed rangers walk among the herd, shooting the mortally wounded. Then there is silence. For many months, other herds will come to this place, touching the remains of their cousins with the tender lips of their trunks, mourning the dead.

That is a cull.

According to the Oxford English Dictionary, 'cull' is defined as *'selective slaughter of inferior or surplus animals'*.

'This cull was necessary', says the park director. 'There are too many elephants in the park, so we cull a certain percentage every year.'

And how are the elephants chosen for the cull? What marks a herd as the one condemned to die?

The director shakes his head at such naivety. 'We shoot them at random', he says.

The high up bankers

One morning a top banker came in. I could tell he was different straightaway. His freshly laundered suit looked both exquisite and comfortable, and his shoes were handmade. His body was expensively toned and his hands exquisitely styled.

Claire and Ethan had departed on a mysterious mission. Since I was sitting right next to the Front Desk, the top banker mistook me for the person in charge. He started explaining his job in a distinguished upper class American accent. He looked at me as if I was a person.

I felt terribly confused but rose to the challenge, writing everything down and commenting politely on his early presence. He nodded, actually considering my words.

'I've noticed that it's not a good idea to come in here between 8 and 9AM', he said. 'Lots of upheaval and nobody there.'

I nodded, trying to do it as suavely as he did. It made me dizzy just calculating the rungs of hierarchy between me and him.

At this moment Claire rushed back from whatever she had been doing and snatched the document out of my hand.

'I'll take care of it', she said to the top banker, who gave a little bow to both of us and disappeared.

Naughty thoughts popped up. Only a few months ago I would have had no trouble talking to this guy on an equal footing. I was a child of democracy and egalitarian policies. 'All men are born equal', I was constantly reminded, and now, all women were equal, too.

But here, inside the Most Successful Bank in the Universe, I could barely stutter. The Social Darwinist experiment was working. I had adapted to my position in life and proved all those right who had put me in my place.

Occasionally I saw other top guys in the lifts. We rode the floors in awkward silence because nobody was supposed to talk about business in the steel box. I'm sure they wished they had their own lifts. Maybe, if the Bank did really well one year...

I also heard that there was a whole floor, the famous Fifth Floor whose entrance was locked against all comers and who shared nothing with us except the fire stairs that were of course exit only and allegedly contained the most stylish office furniture in London.

There were whole separate meeting rooms with waiters and all day buffets, too, rumour said. This may well have been true, and then again maybe not. Like Peter's kiss, the whole thing may just have been a graveyard fantasy.

(Peter's kiss was real. I knew that. But sometimes, just before dawn, I doubted my own memory.)

On the other hand, the company wide emails from New York were signed off with the top boss' first name as if we were personal friends. We were encouraged to call him Tom any time we met him. The emails always ended with an affirmation that people were the firm's capital and that they treated us well because without us they would be nothing. Culls were never mentioned.

Another time I saw a top banker inside one of the glass walled offices talking down to younger one who swore at us ferociously every night. I couldn't hear what he said, but he was leaning over the young banker's desk, his mouth almost touching his ear.

The young banker was looking at the carpet and I saw that his hands, hidden under the desk, were shaking. I wondered if this top guy had a distinguished upper class American accent, too.

The C word and the F word

Once again, lying on my bed in the afternoon, I couldn't sleep. And neither could I keep away from the naughty books.

Philosophers of the enlightenment and 20th century historians were corrupting my mind. I read and re-read John Stuart Mill, Habermas, Foucault, Hannah Arendt… Books that I read or should have read during my studies and practice of anthropology.

And what I read looked very different to me now.

Some of these books kept me awake in fear, others sent me to sleep after a few pages.

When I bravely went back to the classics though, I was in for a bit of a shock. Plato's 'Republic', written 2,500 years ago, was actually a pretty good text book for the kind of system we were under at the Most Successful Bank in the Universe right now. The main difference was that Plato's elite group of philosophers who were destined to rule the state and everyone else (to the point of selective breeding), had been replaced by the elite of our natural leaders. Though to be fair to Plato, he never killed the elephants.

Once again, corrupted and naughty on my afternoon bed, I was flirting with the F word.

I couldn't help thinking how the concept of the cull, both in its imagery (making us into inferior animals) and its execution (and execution was the operative word here), was part of the proto-fascist ideology.

The crypt

And then on another early Sunday morning, waiting out the period between my short shift and when the tube would start running, it rained, hard and cold, drenching me through my jumper before I had even walked two steps into the graveyard.

The inconspicuous door sat flush in the smooth wall of the Bank. No way I could go back in – security would have been suspicious, and my second entry would have shown up on my pass, to be questioned at any point.

So I put my bag on my head and raced towards the dark outline of the crypt.

It was a small crypt, as crypts go. No longer attached to a church, it really was little more than a marble shed at the back of the graveyard, but it did have a protruding roof. To shelter who or what? To shelter me, that morning, from the rain.

I knew that the ghost walks often stopped there, in the evening, when the crypt threw shadows over the surrounding gravestones, and sometimes an out of work actor would appear in a Victorian costume, searching for his dead love… (Ghosts no longer wore sheets, not even for tourists.)

The crypt had a black door, not unlike the one that led into the Bank, but it was always locked. It turned out to be locked that morning, too. But there was a slit at the top of the marble walls, leaving them just short of the roof (maybe for the wind to blow through?) and just high enough for an enterprising graphics operator to look over if she stood on her tip toes, and see what was inside.

Even with the rain, the light was much brighter in the graveyard, and my eyes took a moment to adjust.

That crypt was full of coffins. I hadn't expected that. Coffins stacked up, disintegrating, and rotting into one another. Instinctively I drew back. Was that safe? Presumably, if the City of London allowed it (although of course it WAS a public institution and as such hardly reliable).

Then I reminded myself: even if John Ambersand was still resting underneath my feet, the time of the plague was long past. Hundreds of years in the past.

I rose to my tip toes and looked again. Coffins. Yes. Only wood. Old wood. I couldn't see anything else. Perhaps the coffins were empty?

My eyes travelled further into the shadows and stopped. Oh no.

I wished I hadn't seen that but it was too late.

The coffins might be empty, but their erstwhile passengers had just moved a few yards away.

Skulls were stacked along the wall of the crypt.

Bones covered the floor.

I dropped to the soles of my feet, tucked the bag under my elbow and ran. Rain or no rain, I didn't want to stay here.

The rain took me at my word and didn't relent. By the time I hit the street I was shaking. My hands were ice cold, and my jumper rubbed heavily against my skin.

So many people had died here. So many had lived short, painful lives.

Before the shadows came again. I wanted to live!

3AM ardour

Around 3AM my feelings started to get intense. If I was sad, I would get sadder. If I felt suddenly mellow I wanted to embrace the world. If I felt attracted to someone…

And as the clock crept on to 4AM I felt that this someone was right here. The same someone who had flirted with me on the tomb stones and who had kissed me in the little passage behind Cobblemaker's Lane.

Right now he was sitting a few desks over, working on a shared project that involved constant passing of Pages down the lines.

I could hardly keep myself from running up to the shift leader (Ethan tonight, substituting for Claire on a trial basis) and begging him to let me be on Peter's team. That way his fingers would touch mine, again and again. Sparks of enchantment.

Such feelings were common on the graveyard shift. Sleep deprivation impairs cognitive functions, and impulse control goes first.

Our little niche

I managed to time my 4AM break to his, and suggested a vigorous walk around the Field of Desks with our cups of tea, just to get our circulations up against the cold.

Peter didn't know this but a few nights before I had discovered a tiny niche just opposite the Spanish team, a cul-de-sac with no discernible purpose, not overlooked by anyone.

When we passed, I slipped into the corner.

'Come here', I whispered. 'No one can see us.'

Peter turned around, surprised.

I stuck my arm out and grabbed him.

Peter laughed and put his tea cup on someone's desk. Then he leant back and let himself be pulled into the niche. It was just big enough for two bodies, if they squeezed close together. We kissed. And then again. And again a few times.

Peter was a good kisser. Definitely. I reached up and pulled his head down just one more time. Yes. Soft lips, agile tongue. His hands were a little further down, holding my waist, exploring up my blouse...

It lit up my night.

But not so much that we forgot the legal limits of our eye breaks.

Suppressing wild giggles, we split up and made it back into the Center from different directions in under six minutes. Well, he did because I was a gentleman and let Peter go in first. Thirty seconds later I endured Claire's reprimands like a little lamb and promised to only take four minutes for my toilet break in two hours' time, a promise which I kept. All things are possible to those who know a secret niche just big enough for two.

At 5AM, looking at him, my eyes filled with tears.

I was struck by a terrible wave of despair, only relieved,

but not much, by the miserly grey dawn that rose inside the rain. Yes, it was a new day, yes, the world went on, but what did it help me?

Luckily some bankers came and complained about their jobs.

6AM is not short shifting

'6AM isn't short shifting', said Claire.

She was talking to her retinue (Peter had started to call them her dogsbodies but only from a safe distance) but her voice, raised as always, broadcast the message across the room.

'I mean 6AM is only two hours anyway but actually it's only one and a half hours if you took half an hour's break but actually you could take one hour's break. You could. So then 6AM is only one hour early. That's not really short shifting. Short shifting is 4AM.'

I forced my eyes down to the keyboard. I remembered that 'we don't take breaks on this shift'. I still had to choose, every two hours, whether to go to the toilet or to the kitchen. I still had a quarter of an hour subtracted when I was coerced into making tea for 20 people.

'But really it's two hours', said Ethan. He sometimes, suddenly, took the underdog's side, exuding fairness.

I thought that 2 times 4 was 8, so that meant if I was short shifted at 6AM every night I would lose the pay for one whole shift. A quarter of my weekly income.

Luckily no one could hear my thoughts as long as I didn't voice them. Claire's dogsbodies were still standing around her, making little confirmatory noises.

Everybody else was silent.

'So, you, see', the loud voice went on, 'you're not really being short shifted.' I understood and packed up. Luckily the underground started running at 6AM except at the weekends so at least I didn't have to pay for a taxi as well.

Ethan smiled. His little game had not damaged him at all. I was never sure if he thought he was cleverer than Claire, riding on her obvious soft spot for him, or if he was taking out a little bit of an insurance policy, just in case things ever changed around here. Not that they would. As far as anyone could see, this was the Eternal Empire.

A few mornings later I was walking a little too fast down the corridor shortly after 8AM. It had been very busy so we all got a full shift. I nearly ran into Claire and Des.

Luckily I was able to slow down at the last moment. If it had been in the street, I could have looked at shop windows but being in the Bank the corridors were blank. I just had to hope they wouldn't notice me.

'You know', Claire said, 'this is the first time that I've been able to get off work on time. Most mornings I'm there until much later. Yesterday it was 9AM.'

'Oh that's so tough', said Des.

I never calculated Claire's probable income but if I try to make a guess now I would think that it must have been close to twice the amount of mine, at least most weeks.

Still waiting

Of course I said nothing.

Every night, we were waiting for the cull.

It must be close, summer was nearly gone.

The best and brightest

I came across him one breakfast morning in the newspaper.

My head was heavy, my eyes unreliable.

I didn't recognize him from his picture because I had never seen him. But I could call him any time, and by his first name too.

'He is typical of this company of the best and brightest. The quality of its employees is the real reason why it is so exceptional, so successful.'

I looked as closely as my dry exhausted eyes would let me but this was not an ad. It was an article. The paper was highly regarded, even thought of as intellectual.

In moving words the article told the story of a young man from a disadvantaged background who was awarded a scholarship at Harvard for his exceptional brightness. There, he and his special talents were discovered, no, 'hand-picked', by the bank. Or rather, the Bank. The Most Successful Bank in the Universe. The one I worked at.

I swallowed my egg toast whole.

This article was about Tom. My friend Tom. Tom who sent me weekly emails. Tom who encouraged us to call him by his first name, should we ever meet him down a corridor.

'This bank is different from all others. Simply put, they are the best in the world.'

This was the highly regarded newspaper's highly regarded opinion, not Tom's.

'Everybody knows that', said Peter that night. Ilya said he had known it too.

(Claire didn't comment. She didn't really read much.)

I looked at the field of desks and decided to rely only on my own observations. Of course I kept it to myself.

Sinking

So I sank into the Center.

I got used to sleeping in the day. I discovered that I had to treat sleeping as an appointment to be scheduled in my diary, rather than the period of non-time after midnight it had been before. It became a rendezvous with my dreams.

Luckily I was able to afford the expensive foam ear plugs now. I relished the feeling, standing in the pharmacy, making a choice based on function and quality rather than on price alone. Whenever I looked at their cheerful orange colour, I felt rich and in control of a least one aspect of my life.

I slept with the curtains open to welcome the sun into my dreams.

A long line of working midnights stretched out in front of me, but it was a life with enough money to survive. Eat, sleep, breathe – for the moment, it seemed enough.

The first cull

Many of the angry young bankers I had worked with were culled that month. I felt nothing. They had never told me their names.

Interestingly, according to Claire, not as many, proportionally speaking, were fired from the Center. Only about twice the number that would have disappeared over the course of a month or two anyway.

'They're building it up, they need the numbers', said Ethan sourly. He looked disappointed and later I saw him stuffing coins into the Sweets Machine.

From our training group, only one person was culled. Rita.

Ilya told me during a handover where he managed to accidentally pocket my electronic pass (which later made it impossible for me to reach the toilets without outside intervention and led to a rather lame apology the next night).

I tried to remember if I had noticed any signs. Rita had been criticised more harshly and severely by Lucy than any of us, that much was true. Almost every night she was sent to read her best practices and report back what she had learned, standing in front of the raised desk.

'She was fired for being incompetent', Ilya said, 'and for dressing inappropriately.' I was more and more impressed by his secret sources. But then he was there during the evening shift and who knew what was going on there? It was a different country.

'Hmmm', I said. At least as far as the dress code went, hadn't Rita adapted and conformed? Wasn't that what they wanted? Wasn't it unfair to be fired for an offence she had rectified, for wearing frumpy skirts over your leggings when all you wanted to do was to show off your legs?

But then, of course, she wouldn't have been given an official reason. Not during the cull, and not anyway. She would just have got the call from the agency not to come in tonight. No personal stuff to collect since we didn't have our own desks, no walk of shame between two rows of security. It was only owing to Ilya's superior sources that I got to know the truth.

I wasn't going to say I was sorry. I didn't like Rita and she didn't like me. I had seen her suffer, that was true, but what if she had been taken up and promoted by Claire? I was glad Rita never had a chance to become a shift leader. I shivered at the thought, then felt bad for thinking ill of those who had passed away.

Ilya watched me closely, then lifted his backpack. He winced a little.

'Bites into my hand', he explained.

'Oh', he said over his shoulder as I slipped into his still warm seat, 'and of course she didn't pass her three months' assessment.'

Assessed

Only a week later I had my own. One night I was ordered to come in at 10PM next day and report to the Third Basement where our old Trainer was supervising the event.

I took two coffees and all my courage, I walked down the carpet strip tunnel between the half opened boxes lining the meter thick walls.

At least tonight I was only shaking from fear, and not from hunger and exhaustion. I would be able to buy breakfast after this, whatever the outcome.

In spite of these brave thoughts I didn't sleep much during the following week.

Every night could be my last. Then, one midnight, I was called in to see the Head of Training, just before she went home. She was sitting in one of the nice glass walled offices at the outer rim of the floor that belonged to some unsuspecting middle rank banker. Apparently that was a perk of the evening shift, for those who could make it happen.

'You passed', she said.

I passed! I passed.

Not only was that morning's breakfast safe, so were many more.

I didn't hear what else she explained and apologized on automatic pilot for the few mistakes I had made. I passed. Of course, nothing is certain in this life and in the Bank but for now, I was still here.

I had actually planned to go home and sleep immediately that morning but instead I went out and bought myself a superior music device. It was eminently programmable except that I didn't know how to turn the stereo earphones into mono, so when I used it I had to hide my second earphone underneath a pile of tissues stuffed into an empty styrofoam cup. This was a fragile construction that often fell apart when I or a visiting banker made an unpremeditated movement on the narrow desk and then I had to be quick to cram it all back in or the tinny sound coming out of it would annoy my neighbours and, depending on how powerful they were, cause them to bring down the wrath of the shift leader on me.

But I didn't care. From now on, I would have my own music.

Curves

Now I was sometimes given a longer job. One that you could really 'get your teeth into', as Des said. He had been sent on some special courses and was regaling the Saturday night shift with titbits from the higher wisdom of S&I (those that he was allowed to divulge to the masses). There were some upsides to being on that Saturday shift, I had to admit.

For many hours I followed the heartbeat of share price graphs, adjusting their axes and adorning them with 'call-out boxes' explaining sudden reversals in fortune.

At 400%, the lines seemed like rivers. Sometimes I gave in and dreamed of strawberry fields…

At 100% the rivers receded. But I noticed that all the curves had one problem in common: It was really difficult to squeeze in the text boxes in the top right hand corner. That end of the graph represented the future on a time line (the x axis) while the past started on the left, where the x and y axes meet.

The problem arose because all the curves went always upwards.

Sometimes very steeply, so that the proportions of the

chart had to be adjusted and re-adjusted to accommodate these enthusiastic mountaineers.

Shares, profits, forecasted real estate prices, whatever they were (in $bn, of course), the future was always high and rising.

When the icy wind blew from the air condition and I huddled close to my tea cup, when I was so tired that I was grateful for the huge chair holding my body in an iron embrace so that all I could move were my arms and my eyes, when the bankers themselves were close to tears from exhaustion and peer pressure, even then, the curves still always went upwards.

How was that possible?

So one night when they were clustering around me, somehow not unpleased with my work and too tired to argue much, I asked the bankers.

'What are the curves predicting the future based on?' I said.

'Well', they said, startled at this kind of question from a non-banker so low down the chain that one couldn't really expect much cognitive activity from her brain, 'this is forecasting. The curves are based on our calculations.'

'Thank you', I said politely, 'can I ask: what are your calculations based on?'

'Well', they said, 'obviously, the formula.' Shaking their heads at such ignorance but in a way relieved, too. I had just set their world to rights again.

Oh, I knew the formulae. We all did. They were monsters lurking in the computer network, ready to swallow anyone who approached them.

The bankers' formulae filled huge excel sheets that often collapsed under their own weight and had to be rescued by the IT department. Sometimes they sprouted tentacles of circular errors that sent you into a deathly spiral of mutually assured destruction.

I continued on my quest and asked, very nicely, if they could tell me what the formulae were supposed to express.

Surely, even if too complex to be understood by all but the best and brightest, the data must come from somewhere.

It was 5AM, and we had all been there forever. Sleep deprivation lowers the barriers. Prisoners confess, lovers cry, mothers doubt themselves. One of the bankers broke down and admitted that the formulae themselves were based on 'legacy'. Copied and re-copied, constantly refined and adapted to ongoing complexities.

'Ok', I said. That was interesting information, to be sure. It seemed that the formulae had a mysterious life of their own, unknown even to the bankers who serviced them.

Dawn was not far away.

'But', I continued, 'this doesn't really answer my question.'

They looked at. They had told me all they knew.

'My question is: where does the original data, the data that the formulae use to predict the future, actually come from?'

A big sigh went through the bankers' bodies.

'Oh', they said, on their way out, 'they're assumptions. Of course.'

Assumptions.

Who else made assumptions to predict the future?

Images came to my mind.

Intoxicating fumes, ancient symbols on playing cards, chicken intestines.

Witches, magicians, psychics, priests and diviners.

Fortune tellers.

Since no one had told me, even now, I had to guess: Was this the business of the Bank?

Escape to the niche

I panicked.

The Bank, so solid with its metal walls and internal escalators, was floating on a great vortex of nothingness.

In my next eye break I ran and grabbed Peter. I dragged him into the niche, never mind who might be looking.

He laughed but quickly scanned the Floor. He did mind, it seemed.

I kissed and held him close to drive out the terrible vista of the vortex.

My heart was still racing when I came back, and I made many mistakes in my document.

But then the deadly weight of the isolation ward descended on me again, and I numbness spread all over my fears.

Nothingness? Who cares.

Tea bagged

Only a few nights later, on a large weekday graveyard, we were running out of work and looking a 5AM short shifting in the eye.

Still on the last legs of my job, I noticed a commotion at the front desk. Claire and Ethan were huddled together with Lucy. Lucy looked around and then called in Des. Des was definitely destined for advancement. They were keeping it down for once but the low volume of their conversation reeked with intensity. With my one naked ear I could hear little explosions of 'outrageous', 'typical', 'too much', and then the feared, the fated word 'crack down'.

I knew how fond Claire was of this expression.

'They are going to crack down on that!' (whatever the crime of the moment happened to be from using the toilet too often to maiming the footnotes with the wrong fonts).

'They' meant the authorities, invisible to us in the glass offices of daytime. But the people who actually implemented those crackdowns, and the people who reported our infractions to the invisible manager were much closer to us. They were right here.

We pricked our ears and waited. There wasn't really much else to do. It would come. Soon.

And indeed it did.

Suddenly, and without a word to any of us, Claire and her dogsbodies walked out among the rows. Looking down on our desks, sweeping their hands along the rims. We were just as silent. If this went on for much longer, the mice would come out, thinking we'd all gone home. It was hard not to look up when Claire stopped next to you, so close you could hear the breath filling her lungs. And the carbon dyoxide swishing out. While we were holding on to our air. The only thing we could not be denied.

Something was up. Something new. We tried to appear busy and invisible at the same time. Not an easy feat to achieve but we were well practised.

Claire took up a commanding position underneath the South Window.

'Now we'll see, won't we', she said.

Des and Ethan stood ready at the opposite end of the rows. Yes, definitely, something new. They pulled out the paper bins next to each row – large plastic containers that stood at hip height and were, at this time of night, bulging with the hundreds of printouts that had somehow not met the standard, and started to excavate their contents.

As more and more Pages landed on the surface of two empty desks up front, the silence continued. I knew I had to contain myself. Next to me, Catherine, who had still to say more than one sentence to me, took short shallow breaths. I knew she was prone to hyperventilating, there had been an incident only last week. And now we didn't even have a paper bag. I breathed soothingly in her direction. Maybe she could pick it up by bio feedback.

The Center had a dual waste system, which meant several paper bins and one dedicated food bin. They were all the same colour, and of course we had never actually been told about the rubbish arrangements, but everyone soon found out when they made a mistake. The main offence was sinking tea bags into the paper bins which liquidised the documents and was just generally very disgusting. Many many exhortations were delivered on the low morals of those who committed this crime but the practice never changed. I knew why: disposing of the tea bags correctly meant either getting up from your seat and walking across the room (taking expensive minutes of working time away from the Bank) or keeping the damp teabag on your desk until your next eye

111

break (very messy, potentially lethal for your keyboard, and what if you forgot?). Although I am an avid advocate of recycling, I never ratted on a fellow operator. It was just not possible.

Now, the tea bag delinquency seemed to work in our favour.

The Pages were pulled from the waste (Des and Ethan were in it up their elbows, showing potential leadership traits by doing the necessary, even if it was distasteful) and closely examined. Some Pages were then lined up on the empty desks, while others piled up on the floor. However, quite a few of the selected printouts were soggy, and some had big brown splotches on them. Splotches that obscured the automatic identification tags on every Page, showing who had last worked on it. Tea is an excellent dye.

But that did not obstruct the investigation. On the contrary, it spurned our nascent leaders on.

'They are revolting', said Des, shaking out a partly liquidized Page with his furthest fingertips. Did he mean the Pages or did he mean us? Tiny brown drops splattered the floor. And seeped into the carpet.

'You sometimes wonder if they do this at home', Ethan agreed.

'What they need is a good crackdown', said Claire, still leaning against the South Window. He back must be very cold but she also showed the determination of the leader, putting the interests of the Bank above her own physical comfort. Her tongue darted in and out.

And we were sitting right there, trying to breathe, but not too much, only a desk's width away.

This meticulous collection of what would surely turn out to be evidence against us lasted almost hour, during which none of us were sent home. We might be disgusting, but at least we had another hour's pay under our belts.

In the end, after the exhibits had been laid out to their satisfaction, Lucy (who had been too immersed in her S&I duties up on the platform to participate in the bin action except by nodding sternly at us now and then) and Claire carefully sorted through the papers spread out and slowly drying on the desks.

By then it was clear that they were looking at the upper right hand side, where the company ID of the most recent person to work on the document was preserved in the printout. A muted but very serious discussion followed with frequent referrals to the IDs. Lucy and Claire studied the Pages, while Des pointed out the relevant areas on the Page (as much as they could still be identified). It looked like a scene from 'The Boys in Blue'. No CSI necessary, the IDs were our DNA.

Ethan handed over the list he'd been making to serious nods by Claire, who showed it once more to Lucy for confirmation.

My neighbour couldn't contain her breathing anymore and started the funny little hiccups that often preceded an episode.

Then Claire spoke.

'You've been taking advantage, haven't you. It's unacceptable.'

She looked round while, irrelevantly, 'Project Runway' came into my mind with the designers all lined up to hear their fate. I almost expected Claire to say 'If I call your name, step forward.'

My neighbours hysterical mood must have rubbed off on me, rather than the other way round.

Of course, Claire did not utter the famous words coined by the supermodel, although I did wonder for a moment if this was where the inspiration for her hair sculpt came from.

She walked among the rows of desks, studying Ethan's list.

One by one, the culprits were identified. 'I'm holding you back', Claire said. 'Wait for your turn.'

Lucy was already standing in the entrance of the Center, ready to take the first one to an unoccupied office behind the glass walls.

The rest of us were summarily short shifted. (Or not, as Claire said, even that morning, since six o'clock wasn't really short shifting.)

My neighbour and I breathed a sigh of relief together. We were happy to take the loss of pay over the potential loss of our job.

We packed up in record time and were on our way, time sheets in hand to be signed out, when stepped into the narrow entrance, ready to turn the stampede.

'Not so fast', she said. 'First you pick that up!' She pointed at the heaps of discarded paper surrounding the empty bins. Well, empty except for the dregs of tea bags and other indefinable debris.

I suppose, even then, some of us must have shown incredulity on our faces, hesitation in our body language.

But Claire didn't budge.

'You messed that up, you put it back', she said. 'It's your own fault. Next you'll use the food bin.'

For a moment we stood. I suppose to an observer from a different galaxy it could have looked like a face off, but there was no contest. Claire had the power to sign (or not sign) our time sheets, and her signature was the only way to get that night's pay. The work floor was empty except for us, our invisible managers still asleep in their invisible bedrooms.

'It wouldn't be fair on the cleaners, now, would it', said Claire. She never knew how to leave a good thing alone. But then she didn't have to.

So, yes, we picked up the soggy paper and stuffed it back in the bins while our colleagues were taking the walk of shame to the private office and a 'good talking to' by Lucy from S&I.

Yes, I did that for the money, too.

The crime, I heard through the rumour mill during the next graveyard shift, was a huge accumulation of negligent operating and disregarding of Page rules over several shifts which had led to a final document disgracefully out of tune with the company style guidelines. Luckily Lucy had spotted this in her QC before it went out. S&I had saved the Bank.

Peter was one of culprits, but he never told me what happened to them. The only thing I knew was that they were seen studying their best practices in the following weeks and taken out by S&I at irregular intervals. Did they get a black mark on their company records?

'Well', said Ilya, 'at least they were not fired. The Bank must really be desperate for people.'

One night when no one was looking I took my teabag and squeezed it all over the print outs in the paper bin. I felt terribly guilty and it went against all my ecological principles but I felt compelled to do it. Nobody saw me, or if they did, they didn't tell.

What money can buy

It took a long time, but at some point I had a little money left over every week. I owned new shoes, and new skirts. My book shelves were repopulated (little by little) with second hand science fiction paperbacks that provided hours of comfort in a succession of alternative universes. A new coat could wait. On a trip to Brighton, I saw a pretty pink handbag and I bought it. It swung along my hips as I walked to the underground station at night. I had my weekly travel card and I never struggled to pay the rent. Soon I would be able to start repaying my debts.

It was amazing how money helped me sleep. The knowledge that the basic necessities were covered took the edge off, even in areas of my life that weren't directly related to money.

Gradually, I grew bolder. I chose between strawberries and raspberries in the supermarket, just on the whim of the moment. I signed up for a yoga class and smiled when it turned out to be far too advanced for me. I gave birthday presents. I collected pretty brochures of classes I could take.

And I discovered that, on some days, I could look at the files of my old passion and not feel too much pain. For me, anthropology was in the past. One day, soon I would be able to admit that my life in the humanities was a youthful indiscretion. We all have our dreams, and we all wake up... Maybe I just needed to study some more. Something more useful, like Ilya and Peter. I read course brochures in bed in the morning and on my off days in the park. And all of this good fortune I owed to the Bank.

Here tonight and gone any time

Ilya had gone part time on his course.

'It will take me three years now', he said, 'but I was just getting too exhausted, working evenings, lectures and homework in the day. It was hard to find a study group with my hours, as well.'

I certainly understood that.

'My wife is disappointed, though', he added. 'She was hoping for the big money. And for me to come home before 1AM every night.'

The tele-marketer from our training group with the upstairs connections who had gone onto the day shift had successfully short tracked it to a supervisor position, he said. We looked covertly towards the towering raised platform. Just in time to see Lucy hand over to Des for his first solo graveyard.

'And he's made it, too', I said.

Ilya looked at me with pity and got up to vacate his seat.

'Lucy's been called to New York', he said, 'and, oh, Peter's leaving at the end of the week.'

Crumpled little number

I didn't know.

Apparently, kisses didn't count when it came to leaving forever. Maybe he thought it wouldn't make any difference to me. Maybe he didn't think of me at all. Maybe we had never kissed outside my head.

In my eye break I went and looked at the niche opposite the Spanish country group. At least that was still there. I touched it. Architecture was my witness.

I tried to imagine the Center without Peter and found that I couldn't. How had that happened? We hadn't even had coffee together, properly. A few months ago I'd never heard of the man. Personally, I blamed the graveyard shift. I didn't want to blame Peter.

For several nights I agonised whether I should or should not give him my phone number before he left. I wrote it down on a piece of paper and folded it over twice, then slipped it under my book. I don't know why I was so super cautious. Even if someone found it and read it out loud to the whole Center as Claire had done the week before with Coco's book of low fat recipes, what was I worried about? No reason why I shouldn't have my own phone number on me, right?

A few times I took it with me on my eye breaks and then Peter wasn't there. So there was no one to give it to and I had to take it back to my seat, slip it under the book again.

By night three, the piece of paper was a little crumpled.

Luckily, I did managed to catch him eventually in the kitchen. I suppose everyone had to go there at some point. It certainly looked as if everyone, who had been on the Seventh Floor during the last 24 hours, had.

'Hi', I said. 'I've been trying to talk to you.'

Peter looked at me as if he had forgotten who I was.

'I'm so tired', he said.

I didn't know what to say so I nodded. Nodding was my one new skill.

'I heard you are leaving', I said, after a respectful pause. I was actually quite cool about it, I thought.

'I am leaving, yes', he said, graciously accepting some milk into his very dark tea.

'I only did this for the money anyway. I never meant this to be a job. I'm going to finish my studies and then I'll be able to earn at least four times as much.'

Was it really that easy? I didn't know. People were doing it, so probably yes.

I'll never see him again, I thought.

'Well you see', said Peter, warming to his tale, 'a few weeks ago I realised, well, my girlfriend and I realised', (He had a girlfriend? Since when? All along? Brand new? I shivered hot and glowed cold), 'when we went through my schedule we realised that I was only getting six nights' sleep a week instead of seven. In the morning I would go to my course, you know, and then I would come home around five and then I would have dinner and sleep a bit, and then go to work on the graveyard. That's for five nights a week. And then I would sleep properly for two nights, Saturday and Sunday. So altogether that came up to less than six nights' sleep.'

He looked at me heroically.

(He had a girl friend? He lived with her?)

'I just have to set priorities', said Peter firmly. 'I want a better life.'

I could see in his eyes that he was going to turn away. Without thinking, I interrupted him.

'Keep in touch', I said and held out my crumpled paper.

He stared at it.

I wished I could have sunk through the concrete down to the Third Basement and underneath into the welcoming earth.

'My phone number', I said.

'Oh, right', said Peter.

He took the piece of paper without touching my hand, unfolded it and looked at it briefly.

'We'd better go', I said.

'Yes', said Peter. He folded the paper up again and put it in his pocket.

Out of habit, I let him go first and took a more tortuous route through the field of desks. I took the reprehensions and penalty minute without feeling a thing.

After that, I saw Peter a few times from a distance but missed the actual morning when he left. I felt very jealous. In a few months' time he would have a glamorous executive life and I would still be here, stuck in endless night shifts, amounting to nothing.

I thought of him every time I looked through the Saturday job ads. I felt he would go for the large ones with corporate logos or even the fancy ads with hand drawn cartoons, the ones where they really wanted you and spent the money that said so. Peter would look back on this year and shake his head and wonder why he ever did this.

I would become a little speck in the dust.

Deskilled – and counting

One two three four.
One two three four.

I counted the Pages of my print-out. I had to be sure.

One two three four.

I couldn't afford to make a mistake. The raucous laughter of a Saturday graveyard was surging in my ears. Claire and Des and Ethan. Coco joining in more cautiously.
'Hahahaha she can't even count to four!!'

I had already forgotten that only last night I had created some very complex charts and used advanced formulae to adjust them.
Dimly, I remembered that I had been quite fluent in mathematics at school.
But that was a long time ago. Maybe it had happened to someone else.

All I knew was that I must get this right, and all I knew was that I would fail. Again. And I didn't want to pay the price of another failure. I just didn't have it in me.

One two three four.

Four. Really? Was it three or was it four?

Maybe I should go back and count all the pages again.
I looked at the clock. I had already overshot my Estimate by at least 15 minutes. Ilya said it was all going into a file on the supervisors' system. Again, I was squeezed in an iron grip between loss of pay and potential loss of job.
Missed her deadline. Miscounted her pages.
Again, I panicked.
One two three four.

If a you are not a leader…

Being battered into submission was painful. I didn't want it. I didn't even want to believe that it was happening. Night after night, I came in thinking that surely, now, it would all be better and that I had been overreacting. Morning after morning, I left feeling like a skinned rabbit.

In the world of the Bank, I was the mud that you kick.

I was a loser, and I deserved what I got.

Hard times

Hard times, I told myself, hard times.

Hard times come and they must be endured.

Hard times, these were simply hard times.

Why didn't I show some leadership skills myself, and did the necessary even if it meant having to dirty my precious mind with disgusting debris?

I hated them but better times would come, if I only go through them.

Somehow, the thought consoled me.

Hope, the eternal endocrinal sauce.

But hope was wrong.

I was wrong.

Hard times? These early times, at the start of my graveyard life, were nothing compared what was to come. I would have done better not to feel so sorry for myself so soon.

Oh no, the hard times, the times that really merited their names, those times were still to come in the Most Successful Bank in the Universe.

SEASON TWO
THE WITCHBITCH

Good morning good night

Sound, scream, fire. Fire! Fire bells, the ones that rang at school. Fire fire! London's burning! Emergency! Emergency!

Where?

Is it too late?

Something clicks under my crawling hand. It's over. No fire now.

Good. Leave me in peace!

Dive down.

Again! Not again! Another one? Oh.

This is no fire.

I struggle up to meet the bell (a ship's bell?) from the deepest depths of the sea. My body is used to a different kind of pressure. If I ascend too quickly I'll explode.

I am bones, muscles, skin. All glued together by pain.

Pulling up an eyelid means lifting weights. Am I a temple dancer picking up feathers with my lashes from molten wax.

I'm pretty sure my eyes are open but it's still dark. Am I blind?

Something over there, something to the right. Oh yes! Yes. Yes. Just shift and push the button.

Light comes out.

Life is good, I am not blind.

I see shapes and colours, I see strange patterns but what is it all?

Vast vaults of memories. My brain gets stuck, it shows a long forgotten room a continent far away. Faded feelings flood in. I sit up and try to greet a long lost morning.

Someone is talking. Things have happened

Information starts streaming back. Fragments don't connect.

My body is ahead of me. My arms are pushing me up.

Someone says it is ten thirty.

I shake myself. Hair flies around my shoulders.

Ten thirty! Now I know what it means. It means I am late.

It is dark. Dark means I have to get up.

I had to get up many times in the dark, long ago. I remember riding my bicycle on the icy roads, illuminated by the light of my dynamo lamp, fading to yellow and then fading out altogether when my legs slowed down.

Something is going to happen. Something I don't want to happen.

It would be nice to slump a little, maybe lie back down again. Music is playing. Something has finished on TV. The face says goodbye. It means that it is really really late. Emergency! Get up! Not down.

Get up and go.

Getupandgo.

I remember a name. Is it mine? What's your name what's your name in the wake up room after surgery.

I remember a face, then another. Mother do I have to go? Yes. Yes! Now!

There is a bag right next to the bed. My foot has found it.

All sorts of things are strewn on top of it. A scarf. An apple. A monthly travel card.

I pause. I'm waiting for someone to tell me, hey, you don't have to do that. Not tonight. Tonight is a night off, remember? You can sink back again and sleep. But the reprieve doesn't come. Go.

I push the rest of my body up and climb over the bag. Gravity is heavy tonight.

Ten minutes. Ten minutes to get ready.

Before memory, is a state of bliss. When it was just my body, my brain and me.

Lugging myself around on clumsy feet, it all comes back. My brain is connecting. It spares me no detail. Mother do I have to! Yes! And go!

Another shift starts at midnight.

Coconut retreat

The bathroom is so very cold. Icy tiles stick to feet. Chill jumps on body. But I must unpeel my sleepshirt. Quick! So cold… The water won't heat up properly, but there's no time. At least the shower cream is coconut. Strong coconut. The bottle promised that it would take me to a South Sea island and if you could travel by steam and smell, we would be there. Maybe the whole island is a coconut.

I don't want to get out. Outside the warm coconut water is the night, the many many tedious tasks of getting ready, and then my journey… And then Claire.

I don't want to think about it. What is awaiting me. Possibly awaiting me. After last night. Maybe it will be forgotten. Things do get forgotten, overlooked.

Not many though. And not on the graveyard at the

Center of Global Excellence.

Maybe if I stay here, under the shower. Inhale more coconut.

Maybe if I go back to bed, call in sick. I've never called in sick, not even when I had the 40 degree fever flu.

Because if I'm sick, I'll get no money. Being sick means no pay. And the 'sick' mark against my name. Big yellow S. To be picked out at first sight. When they are scanning our records for the next cull…

And I will still have to go in tomorrow.

I switch the shower off and scramble out of the bath tub. This towel is getting old and thin. It doesn't soak up enough water. I'll go to work in a clammy skin.

Almost ready

I never think it can be done. I cannot reconcile the person I am now, naked in a towel, coconut brain, and the person I will be in less than an hour's time, fitting into suit and blouse, fitting into a slot in the office, filling a slot in the balance sheet. Won't they realise it's just me?

I look for camouflage. Tights. Tights without a hole. Ok, at least without a visible hole.

Skirt, blouse (washed in real detergent at the launderette), jacket, coat. Shoes!

Oh! I forgot. I forgot I forgot. Race back. Shoes slip off feet. Try not to stumble…

The journey is long. I need my book!

Back to the bed where I read myself to sleep this afternoon. Where is my book! I can't see it. It's not under the pillow, it's not under the duvet. It's not on the little table with wheels that serves as my night stand. I need my book! I need it for protection from the night, I need it to contain my fragile soul. I need because I don't want to remember who I am.

I need the book and it isn't there! It isn't – oh – there it is. Stuck. My book is stuck! Between the bed and the wall.

Stuck and bent into an odd shape. Maybe it was remembering another bed in another continent too. Maybe it was trying to go there, through the wall. I should tease that book out gently from behind the bed but I have no time! And I can't leave without my book.

I pull at it roughly. Out! Out!

Like most of us, it yields to force but doesn't remain intact. The book is in my hands but some of the pages are torn. Luckily I've read those already.

Go! Go! Stuff the bag. Apple, biscuits, travel card. Don't forget the travel card! Just forgetting it once, just once, would take away the weekly discount.

Turn out the lights, go back, because I forgot, turn off the TV. All turned off now? Just go. Go. (Yes mother I am going.)

Shoes. Put on my shoes.

My feet are slow.
Maybe Claire didn't notice. Maybe it will be alright.

No it won't be. But don't make it worse by slow feet. Feet will carry you there right in time, but only if you are fast. If not, you'll have to get up half an hour early from tomorrow. No! Do you understand? Yes.

Feet. Feet carry me.
It won't be alright. But still I go and feet will carry me.

Street light warrior

And now the night begins in earnest.

In my room, yes it was dark, yes I was tired, yes I panicked when I didn't find my book, but I was protected. From outside.

Outside is the night.

After 11PM, the streets around my apartment building are deserted. Occasionally, someone passes by, in a hurry, looking over their shoulder, regretting the decision to come home so late. Really, this is a time and place only for cars. And even they are careful once they slow down.

The wind finds my warm body and forces its fingers inside my clothes. It feels like cold steel on naked skin. Mugged by the wind!

I slip on the slimy surface of our street, pollution mixed with acid rain. The street lights are murky and now the council has started to switch every second lamp off in order to save on its energy bill. I don't think many women voted for that. I often see them execute the same nightwalk strategy I use, diving from street light to street light. Go fast but don't run. It's a longer stretch now. Double the fear.

I work on the graveyard shift. This is what I have to do to get there. That's all there is to it. But there are opportunities for self-improvement everywhere. I've learned from my nightly street walk that successful risk taking relies on experience, realistic assessment and relentless watchfulness. And luck.

Of course I've been followed numerous times. Although I walk quickly, although I obviously know where I'm going, clearly local, and although I look strong and capable from the outside, I am still a woman walking down a dark street at night. Alone. That's enough to bring out the predators.

Sometimes I try to attach myself to a couple or a small group of pedestrians. But they are nervous of me. It's not unheard of for women to be muggers. It's uncomfortable but I try not to care. I need to survive. And I have: so far I've never been injured (attempts were made).

I have fallen foul of accidents, though. Once, my foot got hooked in a cable sticking out into the road. I fell and stumbled into the Center with bloody knees which I cleaned up in my first eye break at 2AM. A few times I slipped on autumn leaves soaked in vomit. Still, I emerged dirty but unscathed.

Sometimes I joke and say that the hardest part of my shift is getting there.

It isn't.

In front of the tube station, the night turns lively. Crowds cling to the entrance. Shouting, shoving and fighting.

I try to slalom between the drunken groups. Twist and bend out of their way. Arms can shoot out, bodies can collapse. Vomit can spout.

I can cope with it all.

Whatever happens, I've made it to the underground station every night.

Wild ride futures

The London underground runs until about midnight. The last train from my station left around 11.30 PM, except on Sundays when trains stopped at 11.10PM, a fact that I regularly forgot in my struggle to get up with the Late Night News.

These 20 minutes are probably an overhang from Puritan times and the authorities, secular to a fault in everything else, are still trying to preserve our virtue from excesses on the Holy Sunday. Unfortunately, far from being a festival of frivolities, Sunday was a working night for me, only with more inconvenience.

On all nights of the weeks without fail, those last trains were crowded to breaking point. I was usually able to cram myself in at our station, but by the time I got to Camden, the ride had turned into an obstacle race through narrow tunnels where the air was loaded up with toxic particles and other passengers no longer resembled fellow humans. Everyone was hot, tired and at the end of their tether. Unlike everyone else, however, I was on my way in to work.

The underground line that I lived on followed a confusing and convoluted design, dividing into two sub-divisions twice during its length. One line went through the West End, and although it was the shorter one, it was also even more densely packed than the other one that went through the City.

Connections on the City Line, on the other hand, were few and far between when the service was already, and often prematurely, winding down.

Every night I had to make executive decisions which I then often regretted. The problem was that my aims, goals and needs were severely misaligned with the aims, goals and needs of the system I was obliged to use. My Bank-induced perception of public service institutions was regularly reinforced by using the underground, particularly on weekends.

For a long time I was astonished at reading the impressive percentages on the performance tables that the Underground printed on colourful posters and that I had ample time to read while waiting for a train. 90% punctuality! Wow. Almost like a Curve drawn by the Bankers.

Then, one day, I read in my breakfast paper that Sunday performance isn't even recorded in the tables of public transport. But at the Bank, the lean and mean private enterprise, my first 15 minute unit of pay would be cut if I was 7 minutes late for my shift.

The London underground cost me hundreds of pounds over the years. And that's even before I factored in the ticket...

Time to run through the tunnel to catch the most promising train of the night. Betting at own risk, with customer's own money.

The last leg

And finally we get there. Let me out, this is my station! Let me out!

Clutching my book, finger between the pages, just in case there's a chance to read two more lines on the elevator, I make it through the ticket barrier, up the old black stairs, and start the last leg of my quest.

Of course, the last leg is always the most difficult. In any race. And this one, of course, is now a foot race.

Coat firmly buttoned, bag clutched in front of my chest,

head already down in anticipation of what awaits me, I walk up the slow hill from Blackfriars. For a moment, an eerie silence holds its breath in the tunnel mouth, and then the wind rises up against me like a wall.

Imagine a lonely traveller, battered by the elements, beleaguered by creatures of the dark, carrying a heavy bag, wet, cold and weary, but determined to reach her goal. Where do you see her?

Somewhere in the wild, I would guess. Where we imagine the harsh weather, the storms roaring roughly around the forest, howling madly across the sea. City climate is thought of as soft, tame, or rather, tamed, feeble, artificial rather than natural, a kind of indoor version of the great outdoors.

I did not find it so, on my nightly forced marches through the City of London.

Coming up from the underpath, I have to lean into the wind and push against it, step by step, weight for weight, my body against the darkness, listing forward at a dangerous angle. (If the wind suddenly stopped I would fall and surely break my neck – 'graveyard worker dead in valiant attempt to reach the Bank' my breakfast paper would write, although probably not on the front page…). Cold seeps in everywhere. Damp assaults my underwear and wrinkles the paper in my bag. I close my mouth, my eyes, I find my way by blind compass.

If you want to see that lonely traveller, just look at me.

'The heart of our city is a desert at midnight', my breakfast paper laments frequently. Have they been here? Have they walked up the hill against the storm, as I do now?

Because I know that there are many creatures around, swimming against the stream of daytime. They have their reasons.

Further up the hill, I'm no longer the only one side-stepping the homeless inside their soggy cardboard wraps and being splashed by high arcs of water from the King's Cross bus. I'm also not the only one being harassed by angry male voices from battered cars slowing to a menacing crawl beside me to come take a ride. 'Minicab, minicab, stop lady, minicab'.

I walk on. I know the inevitable moment when the mounting urgency in the call turns into abuse. 'Get in, get in', 'You need minicab' can flip over to 'Fuck you', 'Ugly', 'Ugly bitch', within less than a minute. Then, more elaborately, and delivered with desperate precision by a driver who knows how to match my walking speed to perfection: 'You are the ugliest woman in London'. Culminating night after night in 'Fuck face', or just 'Fuck'. 'Fuck fuck fuck' mounting in furious rage.

I only wished those streets were deserted.

It was strange how they persisted, night after night, getting turned down again and again – and who in their right mind would get into a battered car with an abusive driver? Warnings were circulated by the police and the Bank's security team, reminding us that people could get raped, robbed, maybe even murdered in those cars. But, most incredibly, it seemed that some of those clever bankers from the Seventh Floor and above were regularly among the victims (of robberies, of course, not of rape). How was that possible?

It was also strange, I thought, how much the intensity of the hatred spewed at me from the cars, and the men inside, still affected me, every night. But it did, it was like corrosive acid on my skin.

On the other hand, I survived it every time.

Meanwhile, my feet kept walking. Up the hill, pushing, pushing, against the wind, against the cars, against the streams of rain and abuse, then turning the corner into a calmer and emptier street.

Along the empty windows of the daytime shops and the posh café whose logo Peter had so proudly shown off on his coffee cup that evening so long ago. (And where was Peter now?) My feet never stopped. They walked me round a few corners more, and, before I knew it, through the graveyard, navigating the tombs and head stones with confidence born from experience, and delivering me, safely, right to the nondescript little door.

Where they stopped, all by themselves, like loyal old

horses. I was there.

Once I found my pass and pressed it onto the smooth surface of the decoder, the nondescript little door next to the graveyard would open and I would slip inside, safe from the street until morning.

Midnight is mine

Inside! Inside!

As I walked through the dark corridor and up the space ship escalator, the evening operators poured out of the Center and streamed in the opposite direction, out into the street. They would now brave the journey home. Soon they would sleep. While we worked.

Living mainly at night, in itself, was not a problem for me.

Even before I worked on the graveyard shift, I always enjoyed staying up late. There are 24 hours in the day and I always wanted to experience them all, not just the standard ones.

I loved midnight as a child, when I was allowed to stay up for special occasions, and everyone said 'it's midnight, it's midnight' in a way that they would never glamorize 8 o'clock. Midnight was when everyone counted down the minutes to the New Year, standing in the snow and waiting for the fireworks. Later, midnight was the champagne highlight of adult birthday parties. I remember the first time I stayed up all night to hear the birds sing, and the light rekindle the colours. To me, that was being truly grown up. Taking possession of any hour I wanted, because they were all hours in my life.

Sometimes I smiled on my way up in the lifts at the Most Successful Bank in the Universe, or when I managed to snatch a brief glance through one of our Four Windows and couldn't help being moved by the beauty of London at night, the streets laid out under me, the dark river flowing through the cityscape, the lights on the bridges sparkling in the water, and the huge night sky above. Even if Claire kept a sharp eye out for dereliction of duty and the unsanctioned taking of eye breaks while sitting at the desk.

Sometimes I smiled because I belonged to a small, select group of people who regularly lived through the hours on the other side of midnight.

And then of course there was the other side of midnight. Dark, but cool. Midnight the hour of ghosts. Midnight in the garden of souls. Midnight, gateway to other dimensions... So many stories, so many movies. Hungry Ghosts pressing their noses against the ice cold Four Windows of our Center.

A little unpleasantness with Claire

Did I say I was a warrior? Maybe outside. Maybe I could take on the mean streets of London and live to tell the tale, but right now, walking up to the Front Desk, the best I could hope for was not to be noticed.

My heart was thumping hard against my chest bone. My face was hot and wind whipped. I tried to cool down and steady up, but I could see Claire from far away across the field of desks and I was sure she knew.

And what was going to happen to me.

Like a child at the dentist I could only plead for the inevitable to be delayed a little. Just ten minutes! Just not now... please...

I took my time sheet up to her – she let me wait a bit, but gave it back to me without a word.

I walked along the row of work stations. This night more than any other I needed a good seat. I tried to find Ilya but he wasn't there. Of all the nights when I needed the kind of first class information that only Ilya could provide...

I decided to line up behind Catherine which turned out to be a slight mistake because, without even looking at me, she prepared to delay departure by meticulously cleaning and ordering her belongings before transferring them to her bag. She was well known for doing that, I remembered. Catherine must realise I was waiting but she never acknowledged my presence, and even less my need to sign in or lose my first unit of pay. Our common fear and humiliation during the tea bag incident had created no bond between us whatsoever. If anything, it made us avoid too much eye contact, in case we remembered.

So many obstacles! And, usually, I overcame them all! Couldn't I be forgiven to forget just one? Well, no. Forgiveness was not company policy in the Most Successful Bank in the Universe.

I leant against the glass of the West Window. Even in my thick jumper I could feel the icy cold slicing through. Was Peter somewhere out there, enjoying his new executive life style?

When my shirt had almost frozen to the window, Catherine finally got up and left.

Over on his elevated platform, Des was settling in, moving the S&I pens around and adjusting the S&I chair to his personal liking. The captain taking charge on our eight hour redeye to New York.

Half past midnight

...and we were close to cruising altitude.

As we signed into our systems, we encountered another strange phenomenon. Or, at least, strange to anyone else.

In the world outside, the date changes at midnight. One day ends, the next begins. Months, years, millennia expire. You can't see it, 23.59 is just as invisible as 00.01, you have to take it on faith, trust the face of your watch or the your computer, but it is so, everywhere. Except in the Bank.

Behind the inconspicuous door in the graveyard, the previous day extends until the start of the morning shift at 8AM. The Bank exists in a time all of its own. It was unsettling, and it seemed impossible. I got used to it.

I went up to the front desk and got my job. Did Claire give me a long, searching look? I tried to be cautiously casual. Not to raise suspicion, but also not to trigger her memory, in case she had forgotten after all. I was allowed to walk back and start working.

That, of course, raised my hope. Maybe it was alright after all. Maybe better not to think of it. Live in the present!

Or at least I could try…

In the Center, a semi permanent order was beginning to establish itself.

Slowly, the memories of the outside faded into the ice cold air.

Some of us were already struggling. They had been hit with a terrifying project or an impossible deadline, they were trying to conceal technical problems, particularly from S&I. Maybe they had had a tough journey in, or a family row, or a debt to be repaid by morning. Or maybe they just hadn't slept.

I noticed a few unfamiliar faces, all lined up in the first row close to the Front Desk. Just under the raised platform of S&I. Maybe Des' face was reflected in their monitors, just as Lucy's had been in mine, on my own first night up, not all that long ago.

Oh, yes, I remembered. Rumour (and, more importantly, Ilya) had said there would be a new intake. And, yes, there they were! Good, I thought, the Bank's business must be looking up. Oh no, I thought, they're a threat to the rest of us. More hungry mouths competing for a full shift.

Maybe Claire felt that way too. Maybe she didn't. As a shift leader, surely, she was safe?

She was pacing behind the first row, looking and nodding, then suddenly leaning over the new arrivals' shoulders, pointing out errors, here, there and everywhere (the poor faces got dizzy from trying to follow Claire's finger) and warning them not to be lazy. And of course not to take breaks. 'You don't get up every hour, oh no you don't', she said repeatedly, slapping the desk between two of them, hard, with her open hand. The girl next to the slapping hand turned chalk white under her make up. I was able to contemplate the scene with a certain degree of detachment. At least it didn't affect me. Right now…

A little later, tea got spilled and Claire was shouting triumphantly, waving her hands in the air, repeatedly demonstrating the offence to the whole room with huge kindergarten gestures and sending the culprit off to get tissues from the toilet. He had to come back as well, without them, because he didn't have a proper Seventh Floor pass yet and the glass doors were impenetrable to him. Claire made it more than abundantly clear that whatever else he was, he was obviously not man enough to clean up his own mess. After collecting a series of rejections, Ethan finally lent the culprit his pass. Then he stayed away too long and didn't bring enough paper. Then too much. The carpet was soaking up tea. The newbies were close to hysteria but swallowed it down. Papers got mixed up and fell onto the soggy floor. Ethan rescued them.

The incident dragged on beyond all reason, but nobody stepped in or stopped Claire. The noise level escalated until it drowned out the symphony orchestra playing in my one earphone.

Des looked on from his elevated platform and made a few careful notes.

Didn't I feel anything, watching this? Had I lost my compassion? My sense of common humanity?

In my mind, I knew that what was happening here was wrong. The fear and despair emanating from those new colleagues was obvious. In my mind, I knew that they mirrored my own fear and despair on that first night up, not so long ago. But I tried not to feel it.

Because, unlike then, I was now part of the silent mass of operators inside the Center who witnessed it all and said nothing.

I found that it was quite easy to be part of that silence. All I needed to do was nothing.

And, really, what could I do? What could any of us do?

Standing up for those newbies would have meant certain dismissal. Even trying to help them in small, secret ways would make life very difficult, if found out. And the likelihood of being found out was very high – there was not a moment's privacy during those eight hours of the graveyard shift, except during the few precious minutes when I was able to close the door from inside a toilet cubicle.

I couldn't afford to lose my job.

If I had felt I could afford that, I wouldn't have done all those shameful things that I ended up doing. Things that concerned me directly.

So it was easy to say nothing and keep my head down when it was all about other people's problems. In fact, deep down and secretly I was almost glad that others seemed to be the main targets of intimidation now. It turned the attention of the bullies away from me.

Because of course nobody would stand up for me, either. Well, when I was the main target not all that long ago, nobody did. Everyone was on their own.

In fact, that night, I began to hope, feebly, that, maybe, with all those fresh new people to dump on, and many new incidents unfolding right now, maybe Claire and Des would forget yesterday's, and my part in it.

Unfortunately, I was very wrong. Memories were sharp and long on the graveyard shift.

I was given a repetitive but complicated piece of work that demanded all my skills and deadened all my thoughts. In my caged body, I was starting to feel different flavours of pain.

My shoulders tensed up and my elbows hit the edge of my desk a few times. I had another cleaning fluid fanatic beside me and really didn't want to risk a border dispute. My neck started to hurt and my feet started to swell up. But the pain was very bearable, and infinitely preferable to the dull fear that shot through me from time to time when I remembered what might still be in store for me, particularly when I came closer to the end of my job.

The relief I often felt when I put the document in the out tray (no S&I check for me now after my three months' assessment, a fact that still felt like the Roman act of manumission, the freeing of the slaves), and embarked on my five minute eye break didn't come that night. One glance at Claire and I knew there could be no escape. Not ever and not tonight.

No escape

My offence was so bad we had to go to a separate room.
'Talk to Des', said Claire.

I went and stood before the elevated platforms.

'I'll see you at 5', said Des, looking up from his file, my file presumably.

The newbies behind me perked up. Someone else was in trouble.

Then they perked down again. Was this good news or bad?

The fear flared up in me, but I managed.

I nodded. 'Thank you, Des', I said.

Claire handed me another boring job that demanded the minutest of attentions, and I walked back to my seat to fear some more.

For three hours, I performed my tasks without flaw.

The eight to fours went home. The newbies didn't know it yet, but they would be short shifted.

I carried on with my job.

When the time came, Des had only to look at me once from his elevated platform.

I rose instantly and meekly followed him out of the Center.

Claire shot me an anticipatory glance. Ethan smirked into his microwave lasagne.

Peter, of course, was no longer there, far away in a Better Life.

Siberia blew from the broken pipes.

Des tried various doors along the glass-encased walls until he found an open office. This one had an individually crafted desk that was obviously meant to be set off by an uncluttered, minimalist environment. Instead it was engulfed by stacks of Books and papers and who knew what else. The Bank had no space for Feng Shui.

Des made straight for the owner's chair behind the desk, a fragile looking construction of metal tubes that fitted very stylishly around his slender body.

I was uncertain. Should I sit? Would it be better to acknowledge my delinquent status by standing?

But Des waved me impatiently to a lesser chair, this one standard company issue. Cleary the minimalist desk and chair were intended for a party of one.

Des had a good reason for wanting me to sit: I knew he did not care for being looked down on (and he was used to the raised platforms inside the Center).

'This is about last night's incidents', he said, and I noticed from his self assured tone that, even in the short time of his tenure, he had become a real S&I man. It must be something you had in you, I thought. Something that could not be learned.

'Yes', I said, deciding to keep it short. From somewhere, probably some long forgotten gangster movie, I seemed to recall the advice that it was best to admit to nothing the interrogator didn't know already. Maybe some secrets could be salvaged.

'Two bankers complained about you', said Des. 'One of them is a VIP Senior Manager. You were very rude to him.'

I was a little taken aback at this. I did remember the younger banker who had been so very angry at me last night. Not in detail, and of course I didn't know his name because he never introduced himself to me, but the stream of invectives and toxic remarks he had spouted at me were seared into my memory.

But - who was the VIP?

'Mr Romero', said Des, throwing me a piercing look. It didn't go quite down to the bottom of my soul, but that was because my soul no longer had a bottom.

I searched my memory.

'On the phone', said Des. Maybe he had watched the same gangster films, but was looking at their advice from the other side. He was also not going to give anything away, at least not more than he could help.

Dimly, a memory took shape. Yes.

There had been a phone call, and I had taken it from my

workstation because Claire had been away and Des otherwise engaged. A banker (who, I now realised, must be the VIP) had shouted at me without preamble and demanded that I prioritise his work over everything else.

I had told him that as far as I knew we had a long queue of jobs and I would do whatever I could to draw my supervisor's attention to his but I could not promise anything.

Apparently, this had been enough. Bad enough.

Mr Romero had taken offence.

'He's a VIP', said Des. 'You can not speak to him like this.'

'I tried to pass it on to Claire…', I said. That was a stupid move. I could see it myself.

'You have all been trained to answer the phone', said Des primly.

Not really, I thought, unless he meant Claire and Ethan screaming 'phones, phones' in shrill chorus while they themselves folded their arms and watched cartoons on the internet.

'Sorry', I said. 'I'm sorry.'

That move was correct.

Des nodded.

'We apologized on your behalf', he said. 'You will be careful in the future.'

I agreed. I thanked him for his kindness. And meant it.

People had been fired for less.

Was it possible that I would get off lightly?

Had I been paranoid in my fear, spoiling a day and a night? Was the Center not really so bad after all?

'And now', said Des, 'to your real offence.'

He pulled up his (or rather, my) file again and read out from it.

'Last night you were on project 'Big Tiger'.'

I cautiously agreed, although the names of projects usually made little impression on my memory. There were so many, and they were all so similar.

'This project was pulled up by S&I. It has an unacceptable number of mistakes.'

There was a silence as Des studied my file in more detail. I wasn't going to say anything. Anything.

No banker, not even a VIP, was as important as S&I and its rules. And nothing could possibly be as dangerous for me.

The only good news was that I definitely was not paranoid.

'Ethan has sent a report to the Manager, and your name will be put on the list.'

What list? I didn't dare ask.

'People have been fired for less', said Des, looking at me again with his soul piercing eyes. Maybe he wanted me to talk.

'Yes', I said. He was right anyway.

But while I acquiesced, somewhere inside me, I could feel the stirrings of a big rage.

It was true that I had been on project 'Big Tiger', but only for about ten minutes. However that was long enough to get my name tag on it. And name tag identifiers, as I remembered only too well from the teabag incident, were all the rage right now, so to speak.

As Ethan had pointed out only last night, everyone had to take responsibility for their work. Everyone. Every time, however short. It was high time some standards were enforced.

A speech whose deeper significance only now revealed itself to me.

Yes, a rage was brewing, but I also felt helpless. So it was unfair, so what? On the graveyard shift, there was no recourse to a higher arbiter than Des and Claire. Our managers remained invisible and would remain so for a long long time to come.

'Much less', Des continued. Much less what? Oh, he was still talking about getting fired.

A flame of red hot fear shot through my body. What was I doing, dreaming of rage and recourse when I might not even be here tonight?

'Yes, Des', I said, as humbly as I could. 'I'm sorry.' That had worked last time.

But I wasn't sorry. I was just terrified of losing my job.

I could feel tears pressing on eyes. It was humiliating to

be in Des' and Ethan's power. It was agonising not to be able to fight back. It was excruciating to think that I might now be fired after I had already survived a cull.

'So bear that in mind', Des went on. 'Your name has been flagged. One more offence and that's it.'

My vision was blurred, but I held on. I was not going to fall off my chair like Ilya's banker.

I nodded.

'You are very lucky. The Bank is building volume right now', said Des. 'I'm sure you've noticed our new colleagues on the shift.' I nodded. Yes to all above.

'So for now, you will study your style bible, I'll send you a list of the pages, and you will report to me every night at 4.30AM on your progress.'

'Thank you', I said.

Des leaned back in the designer chair and for a moment I thought he would steeple his palms together, but he refrained. I nodded. I thanked him again.

Des nodded, too, but in a very different manner. Then he closed my file and opened another.

'You can go', he said.

I got up and he waved me away without looking.

'And remember: keep your head down.'

Dismissed, I closed the glass door behind me. Out of the corner of my eye I saw Des take one of his a little white pills and prepare to continue his duties in the nice tubular chair.

As I walked towards the toilet block, Claire intercepted me.

'I've got a banker waiting!' she barked.

'Go back to your seat immediately.'

It really was like that first night all over again.

The grumpy old WitchBitch

Maybe I should just not come in tomorrow night. Maybe I should not come in for the rest of the week. Maybe I should just – leave… My heart did backflips behind my teeth.

Over the last few months, I had managed to save a little bit of money at the end of each week. I watched that money carefully, each time the slip came out of the ATM. The amount was always a surprise, usually less than I had hoped and calculated from my record of the shifts and units I had managed to accumulate. But even so, it gave an incredibly warm feeling inside, that money in the bank. A powerful anti-depressant, at least until the next shift.

And one day I realised, as I stood in the damp morning street, jostled by angry commuters on the way to their own shifts at the Bank and the banks, that the figures on my ATM sheet, flimsy as a communion wafer, could eventually promise me much more.

In time, and if they continued, and if I managed both to pay my debt off and keep my head down so that I wouldn't get fired, these ATM slips could buy me my own admission ticket to a Better Place.

For several months now, I had flirted with a new field of study, reading the brochures, googling success stories, a specialty that would let me use the knowledge from my anthropology degree. According to my research, this new qualification was well sought after by international companies and perhaps even in the diplomatic service. If my income continued more or less at the same level, I might be able to go for the admission interview, and perhaps even join the next intake.

I would be allowed to pay the study fee in increments from term to term, after I had stumped up the initial admission. And the ATM coupon told me I was close, very close to that goal. If I kept my job, I would study in the day and make money overnight.

Or, of course, I could quit and live on my present savings until I had only three pounds left. That was my choice.

I looked at the figures again, smudged now from my

sweat. If I ever wanted to get to a Better Place, I had to swallow my rage and stay at the Bank.

But since nobody was there to protect me, I had to find a way of protecting myself. The problem was, people outside the Bank didn't understand what I was facing, and people inside the Bank had no interest in helping me. What to do?

Well, I did what I had done most of my life when I needed help – I went to the book shop.

Sociology and political science beckoned, but I resisted their allure. The last thing I wanted to do this morning was to re-consider the F word.

Today it was all about me.

I looked at self help, popular psychology, even serious psychology. Why not?

Because I was very tired I brought a little stool and sat down between the shelves. I picked the books and built little towers that I could reach out to. What I had read, I put back on the shelf. Quite apart from anything else, it gave me a wonderful feeling of luxury, after the empty shelves in my bedsit at home.

My question was: how to survive the present situation and create a better life.

I soon discovered that the second part was a lot more popular than the first.

Still, I ploughed through whatever I could. The towers diminished and soon I had a bit of an overview.

The self help books mostly agreed on one basic premise: I was on my own. The world was the way it was, with or without me. Above all, the one thing I could not do was to change other people. According to the self help books, trying to change the world was a total waste of time. And even quite foolish. What I needed to do was to change myself.

I nodded, in the book shop. Thinking about the Center of Global Excellence, and of Claire, Ethan and Des, and their absolute rule over us, I had suspected as much.

Maybe the study of anthropology and occasional forays into sociology and history had given me a misguided idea of the probabilities of system change. The formation of modern democracy could not have happened without a series of revolutionary upheavals, without constant reform, without the demise of old, authoritarian systems. Maybe I had fallen into the trap of foreshortening history into those moments of progress and change, forgetting how long it took, how fragile these changes often were, and how many generations lived and died without seeing much progress at all.

Even now, we all more or less assumed that freedom and equality would last, but would it?

Well, we also assumed that, at least in Western democracies, freedom and equality was everywhere right not, but clearly no one had told the Most Successful Bank in the Universe. My colleagues and I were neither equal nor free. (And that was as far as I was willing to go.)

Turning hundreds of printed pages that dismal spring, I searched and searched. My life was painful enough to drive me on.

Slowly, sitting on my stool, on a succession of stools over many days while the bookshop emptied and filled up around me like the tide around a hermit crab, I distilled and extrapolated information from whatever I could find.

Although clearly more comfortable with sketching out a better future after I had changed myself, the books did suggest a number of methods for dealing with a hostile environment.

First, I was advised to try to shut it out.

In my mind, I tried to build an imaginary wall, a nest or an egg around me, just as they advised. I could imagine it well, and practised on my days off. Cocooned in my mind egg, I ran through the park. Maybe I just needed to be stronger... But when I was back on my shift, the toxic atmosphere (or 'negative energy' as the books would probably have called it) in the Center wrapped itself around me and swallowed me whole, egg, wall, nest and all.

So then I tried not to let it get to me by offering the path of least resistance. Let it run over me like a river. 'I am the flow. Obstacles are like rocks, they may push me in all sorts of directions but they can't alter my watery nature.'

I worked really hard at this one. It came recommended also by philosophy and religion. I persevered. But however much I tried, after a few hours I couldn't ignore the voices and nasty incidents around me anymore. It felt like acid burning through and into my skin

As a last resort, I tried to follow the advice to convert negative into positive energy – that worked for about ten minutes. It was just too much. My little onboard converter burned out.

The books told me that failure was my own fault. There was nothing wrong with the methods, I was simply too weak, too inconsistent, too lazy to implement them. (An assessment that aligned well with Claire's opinion of me…) I should be able to triumph over adversity, and they provided helpful lists of people who had done so.

I started to wonder what lives the authors of these books were leading. Did they know about people like me, had they ever worked in a job like mine, or did they only deal with corporate culture at the loftiest of levels where jaded executives needed to be reassured that they deserved their privileges?

In desperation I tried to google my way out of the trap. Surely, there must be thousands of people out there like me. I just hadn't looked in the right places. The web, it was true, was full of workplace advice. But when I looked more closely, it was not for people like me. Among the hundreds of thousands of search results, almost all were aimed at 'leaders'.

Leaders.

I couldn't believe it. Those leaders again.

Because at the Bank, it was of course also all about leaders. Tom, our first name CEO, the one who wrote us those weekly pep emails, was our supreme leader at the Bank. Daily he demonstrated his leadership qualities in many different ways. Rumour said he was 'rigorous' in his standards, and he himself said that he was relentless in his pursuit of success. Well, and indeed he had made it to the very top of the Most Successful Bank in the Universe. Leadership didn't get much better than that. Every banker would do well to imitate his example. Every banker wanted to be him.

Further down the ladder, everyone who had any kind of power over others demonstrated his leadership with 'stringent' demands of absolute loyalty and 20 hour face time, and marked his territory with another round of the 300 plus updates of our Books.

And even our shift leaders, well, they had the word 'leader' right there, in the job title.

But what about me? I was no leader.

What was I then? There wasn't even a word for me.

Serious psychology and psychotherapy approached the work place as a kind of secondary environment, vastly inferior in significance to the drama of personal relationships. They offered to help me connect my work problem with the constellation of my family of origin (was Claire a stand-in for my mother?), with deep unconscious motivations and various other valuable forms of insight. Maybe those theories could somehow be applied to my life (and I did wonder if I had started to feel both so much angrier and so much more helpless since that horrible night when Peter had left to pursue his Better Life and what might be behind that), but I could see that the dynamics on my shift and in the Bank were not simply the re-enactment of a nuclear family. Something else was going on here, something unique to a large, hierarchical system with very specific goals and a very specific world view. A system that was both local and non-local and that contained many diverse populations and occupied a significant position in global society. Where were the analyses, psychological theories and coping strategies for someone like me, caught in the complex dynamics deep inside that system?

Did nobody understand how traumatic our experience could be? I felt again that we were cut off from the rest of the universe. If no one recognized my existence, was I still part of the human race?

I did find anecdotes about national heroes who survived prison camps with the psyches intact, stronger and better for the experience. I could only admire them. Deeply. Yes, I thought, it is true. I am no Nelson Mandela. But neither should I have to be! I'm only working in the Bank.

I never found the answer to my question, the advice I was looking for.

Maybe it simply didn't exist.

Many times, many nights I gave up. I fought my way into the Center at midnight and then I became part of it. I listened to the shouting of our leaders, and kept my head down. I nodded. I focused on the music in my earphone. I tried to get as many things right as I could but always expected trouble (and often got it), I bowed to S&I, I tried to avoid spies and informers and I swallowed my anger. But however often I swallowed it, I always had to swallow it again the next night. I tried to use my eye breaks wisely and went to the doctor's for the burning sensation in my often too-full bladder. I took antacids and longed for the morning when I would buy myself a sandwich and relaxed on the train going in the opposite direction to the commuter flow.

And then, slowly, almost imperceptibly, something must have evolved inside me, something that only emerges under extreme pressure, creeping out of crevices inside my inner landscape that I had never explored. (The psychology books had hinted at such things but offered no real guidance.) I'm still not sure how it happened, how that new part of me, or whatever it really was, that part that adapted to the situation in a very unexpected way, came into being. I only noticed when it emerged, fully formed, when it took over and formed a protective shield, when it – well, when the defence mechanism I was trying to learn from outside sources suddenly appeared inside me.

Maybe it had always been there, inside me, sleeping. Waiting for the right moment to come out and offer itself to my desperate arms, like a warm but terrible robe?

One night I was walking towards my seat with a newly allocated job. Claire shouted after me, telling me to pick up my pace, to 'move it' 'double quick', and when I 'finally' got there not talk to my neighbours 'as per usual'. To my own surprise I simply walked on. Another shout, this time just a crude 'hey you' and 'listen, you'.

I stopped. I turned. I looked.

She looked back at me and something was different. I saw it in the way she met my eyes. Before I could react, she took a step back.

Then I felt it, too. For the first time in the Center, I couldn't nod or lower my head. I just looked at Claire.

She stood and watched. I'm sure she could tell how surprised I was at my own response.

I frantically tried to remind myself that it wasn't worth the risk. Why be so cautious all those months and throw it out the window in a strop? But the new persona inside me, or whatever you could call her, was gathering momentum.

Then it spoke. It really felt like that, as if something else was speaking, not me. I just held on.

'I heard you', it said. The voice that carried it sounded bitter and sarcastic, very deep, without any richness of overtones, very different from what I had thought of as my voice until then. 'I will do my best as always. Thank you very much for your advice.' This is not me, I thought, but it came out of my throat. 'It's not really me' would not have been a defence in a court of law. And neither would it have been a defence in the Center of Global Excellence. It was me. Of course. Just a part of me I had never encountered, maybe because I had never been under so much pressure before. Forged in the depth of emotional volcanoes…

In spite of her absolute leadership position, Claire was speechless. I wasn't sure if that had ever happened before either.

She shook her head slightly, as if she was also wondering if she had entered a reality shift. While she was still trying to find her feet on the shifting ground, I turned away from her and walked swiftly to my seat. The new entity had taken possession of my body too, it seemed. My hands, clearly still part of the old 'me', were shaking under the desk but nobody saw. What would happen now?

The unthinkable.
I was left alone.
In the corner I heard someone whisper 'she's so rude', and I assumed she meant me, but it sank into silence. I started on my job. And still nothing happened.

An hour later I saw a tiny grey box pop up on a monitor turned towards me at just the right angle. It said 'miserable old cow'. Ilya had told me the Bank had developed the internal 'webflash' system so that we didn't have to get up anymore if we needed to exchange brief messages or, in this case, insults. I read it, continued with my job and waited for the world to end. Another hour and I was still there.

Nobody talked to me. I put my one earphone in and listened to the World Service. A programme on micro credits in Pakistan, featuring a group of brave women who started a business from a sack of rice.

Of course, at some point, I had to finish my job. And return to the Front Desk.

Claire knew that as well as I did.

Unlike before, when the new strange shape had just emerged without warning, I was afraid now. Would it come back? And, if it did, would it protect me? Or destroy me?

I had no time to dither. If I dithered, I was dead anyway.

So, exactly ten minutes before the expiry of my estimated deadline, I signed out of my job, walked to the front desk, and put it in the out tray.

Claire's eyes bored holes into my back. I pretended not to notice.

Just as my hands released the paper, I thought I heard her draw in air, in preparation for a shout.

I swivelled round.

'What next', said the new persona from my throat. Directly into Claire's face.

The unthinkable happened again.

Claire swallowed her shout.

For a fraction of a moment, she looked disoriented, as if familiar particles had grotesquely reconfigured themselves.

'I'll just take my eye break until you decide', my voice continued and I made for the toilet.

'She's outrageous', I heard behind my back, and, 'you don't deserve to be treated like this, Claire.' But only when I was already on my way.

And, very clearly, rising above the dogsbodies, a single male voice.

'Bitch.'

Was that who I was?

The advice books recommended never stooping to 'their level'. Whatever 'they' did, we must never retaliate 'in kind'. The books were concerned with preserving the purity of my immortal soul, I assume.

Well, too late. I had lowered myself lower than the carpet and guess what? It changed the world.

So I'm going to be a bitch, I thought, spritzing water onto my face over the sink. The shape in me stirred. Had I just called her out by name?

'I'm not surprised she's single', I heard from a distance as I approached the Front Desk after my five minutes. Exact five minutes.

The voice that had made the comment fell silent.

So did everyone else.

I stood and stared at Claire, holding my hand out.

Claire did not look up at me. She reached over to the stack of jobs and gave me a long piece of work without comment or explanation. Or eye contact. A morning deadline which meant I would not have to come back to the Front Desk until the end of my shift. When I took it, she turned away from me even further and looked at the holiday snaps on her monitor.

That was it?

I took the project and never asked questions, making a series of lonely executive decisions which were probably just as good as any advice I could have received either from my leader or from S&I.

I got a full shift. My time sheet was signed without query.

All day at home I stayed up and waited for the agency to call.

Outside the bubble now, and with no access to the strange persona forged in the heat of the battleground, I cursed myself and my stupidity. What was the point of this? Hadn't I invested all this time and all this energy and all these vast volumes of swallowed pride and indifference to the suffering of others and wasn't I eating extra strength antacids this very minute to avoid being fired? I needed this job. Had I forgotten that I did it for the money?

Nothing happened. The call I had thought inevitable never came. Evening fell, and night fell, too, and I was still here. Tired and with stomach acid burning through all the tablets in the box, all the way from my belly up to my front teeth, I was still there.

When I came in, Coco gave me nasty looks from her prime real estate seat under the South Window and Paulo (recently elevated to dogsbody) made a big show of his reluctance to share a job with me but I was still there. Tea was made for everyone except me, but I cared not because I was still there. Claire told a new girl in confidence just around the corner from the smokers' stairs that some people in the Center were extremely unpleasant but not to worry she would look out for her. The girl nodded. Her name was Skinney. Was that her real name? Who knew. Who cared. I was still there.

Night after night, my astonishing new persona grew until it covered me like an exo-skeleton. And it slowly dawned on me that perhaps it was not quite as unknown to me as I had thought. I might have had seen glimpses of it before, both in others and in myself, but when I did, I really didn't like it. Whenever that shape stuck its head out to sniff the air, I had pushed it down as far as I could.

Later, when I got to know this persona better, I understood its name: the Grumpy Old Witch Bitch.

The Grumpy Old WitchBitch was not prized when I was a girl, growing up, in fact it was part of a horror gallery of frightening female images. The nagging hag, the screeching wife, the demanding battle-axe, these were all held up as horror cartoons of what not to become. But the Grumpy Old WitchBitch topped them all.

She was feared and despised. I feared and despised her. I tried my best to bury her long ago.

But in spite of my efforts, she was still there, deep inside me, biding her time, and it took the Bank to call her out.

And she worked for me. The secret of her success, I believe, was the fact that Claire and the dogsbodies knew her, too. And feared her, just like I did. Collectively, our fear was greater than our contempt.

I had no illusions about my situation. This was not the well worn tale of the downtrodden victim finally turning and heroically facing her opponents, and from then on earning their reluctant respect. There was no respect on the graveyard shift, and my tormentors thought very much the worse of me after the appearance of the WitchBitch.

All that had happened was that I had stumbled on a way to get them to leave me alone, at least some of the time, by giving them the chance to distance themselves from the grumpy old WitchBitch, both outside and inside themselves. And it came at a high price.

Before the emergence of the GOWB, every time they assaulted me they won, and that made them feel powerful. Now, they would actually feel better if they assaulted me and then left me partly intact, or even if they didn't assault me at all. I was like a poison plant, not immune from being eaten by a determined goat, but much better left alone because of my ugly smell, appearance and taste, except in cases of extreme famine. (Or occasional needs to 'crack down' on everyone, regardless of personality. And of course that happened, too, more than enough.)

The price I paid for having less pain inflicted on me was being surrounded by the stench of an unpleasant reputation which was passed on immediately to any new person on the shift (and plenty of old ones on other shifts – the telemarketer from my training group who had long since been fast tracked to a supervisor position was rumoured to have predicted this all along all the way from the day shift, or, in fact, from the first moment she laid eyes on me in Basic Training, down in the Third Basement.)

I felt it, I noticed it, I could even smell it myself. I didn't like it and I didn't like the person I had become in the Center.

But thanks to the WitchBitch, I was still there.

Don't try this at home

Most nights, I shifted into the dubious protection of the WitchBitch now. As soon as I approached the Center, I could feel my body change. It became heavier, clumsier, and I could almost imagine ugly outcroppings growing around my back and chest like an insect carapace. I reserved my pretty pink purse for days off.

Still, it was bliss inside. Well, comparative bliss.

Inside, inside my spiky armour and hiding behind my monitor, I had the space and the silence to feel almost like a real person again.

But, dear reader, before you try this method yourself, please remember that I was extremely lucky in the timing and effect of the emergence of this survival shield. It coincided with the arrival of the first batch of newcomers, and soon a second one. These newbies all knew nothing. In the maze of terror created by banker pressure and constantly reinterpretable regulations they could be misled, intimidated and broken down, just as we had been. The newcomers were the easier targets now, and some of them were clearly being marked out if not indeed 'groomed' outright for special treatment. I have no doubt that, in our leaders' minds, this was another process of evolutionary biology in the Bank, let's call it the Selection of the Unfittest to Survive.

Interestingly, the shift leaders themselves could not tolerate being attacked for a single second. They had a very very thin skin of their own (probably beyond the reach of any commercial cream). But they were quite safe here, their protection was their power and retribution was both hard and swift. A proper crackdown.

You see, on the Seventh Floor, there were no heroes.

Fresh blood

The Center was not the only place in the Bank to build up volume. There were now many new bankers, too. The Field of Desks was filling up with unknown faces. I began to understand the wisdom of not knowing their names. Although it was a result of their utter contempt for us, seeing us as a cross between servants and machines, really, what would have been the point? Most of them would not last long in here anyway.

Was this how seasoned soldiers (survivors by definition) felt in a real war, when the young recruits arrived?

Entering my second year at the Most Successful Bank in the Universe, I had already outlasted many, and the next cull was as certain as were the frequent sorties from the trenches.

Sometimes, when I calculated their odds of making it through, and what they were willing to do to get through in the face of the overwhelming statistics of obliteration, I felt compassion for the young bankers. They, too, were here to be broken, to become the scrap heap from which the new leaders would arise, forged in the steel of battle, the strongest of the strong, the rulers of tomorrow and the world. As far as the Bank was concerned, their sacrifice was more than worth it. It was essential to select the Best.

But then I thought of us, the graveyard of the humanities. What about our dreams?

We were broken already, and who cared about us?

Much later, a very catchy label emerged for the distinction between the bankers, both old and young, and the rest of humanity. They were the 1%. We were the 99%.

Starving Ghosts

Flying my desk through the night, I had a feeling that I was missing something that I couldn't name, something forever out of reach. When I looked up all I could see were ghosts, pressing their dead mouths against the glass of the Four Windows. Starving ghosts with big fat bodies.

I filled the void by applying for my chosen course, hoping it would someday lead me to a Better Place. And with the offerings of the Sweets Machine.

Song of the Sweets Machine I

The sweets machine on the Seventh Floor (like her sisters on the Fourth and the Ninth) was not even strictly a sweets machine. It also carried chips and chewing gum in the top two rows. I often saw the bankers in front of those rows, cursing an empty slot of pork scratchings. During the championship season, we sometimes got bags of little footballs filled with cheese.

Yes, I did look at them. There wasn't much else to look at in the Center.

But what I needed was further down.

Show me what you can do, girls…

Number One, come to mama, you deep dark chocolate chunk. Two and Three are our twins, different in name only, with identical smooth sugar hearts coated in chemical almond and cinnamon surrogate. And here's exotic Number Four, oily skin spiced with coconut. Yes, coconut. To scent my tongue, this time. Or shall I splash out and have expensive Number Five, the bag of tiny multi coloured buttons? Some people said the colours all tasted different but that was an illusion. My breakfast paper had discovered that they were all just the same sugar. Who cared? On the night shift, sugar was everything.

I never bought those kinds of sweets in the daytime. I

didn't buy a lot of sweets in the daytime anyway. In the daytime bought fresh fruit. Every night, I brought in the daytime apples my daytime self intended to eat. But later that same night, I was no longer providing for a healthy old age. Late at night, I stuffed myself with the worst kinds of sweets from the sweets machine.

Overflow

There were so many new people now. Week after week, they came up from Basic Training in the Third Basement into the full glare of the Seventh Floor. While the weekend shifts were still relatively small, weeknights became quite crowded, and sometimes there were no seats left in the Center. Because of the Overflow, some of us had to sit at the crosses out in the field of desks.

Who has been sleeping in my bed?

Paulo grumbled every night about the debris left behind on the desk he was told to occupy 'just for now' and rubbed the surface furiously with rolls and rolls of moist computer tissues until he had marked the territory with their scent. The effect was that everything, including his hands and shirt, smelled like a heavily deodorized public toilet. And that smell lingered... But of course, however vigorously he rubbed, he knew very well that no desk was ever his. His tenure would wither like the grass under the morning sun.

The desks outside the Center, unlike the ones inside, were under Permanent ownership (and the owners were never told what happened to their property after midnight...). Like the homes that so many of us were trying to buy, these desks had been comprehensively and thoroughly personalised, often including pens, little bowls with assorted weird looking objects, animal figures of all shapes and sizes and accessorised apologies for long forgotten slights.

After a while, however, it seemed that we had left too

many traces and from then on we were regularly reprimanded for soiling a secretary's desk with our dirty night time presence. I sometimes wondered how they knew, the desks looked the same to me before and after, except perhaps for a few crumbs on the carpet which the cleaning crew at 4AM should have removed anyway. But I suppose after more than a year of hot desking, I had lost the ownership instinct. The arrangement of the pens, the angle of the files, the exact position of old jokes on slowly drying stickers were probably so precise that as much as a dislodged molecule would disturb them.

After a night of rebukes, pens and paperclips always started to disappear from those desks and turn up randomly on the floor. Attempts were made to investigate but in the end it all came to nothing but a lot of resentment among people who never met each other.

The new economy

The Bank was hiring big time.

Rumour was enthusiastic. Rumour was always right. Rumour should have run the Bank and maybe it did.

It was because of the new economy.

The new economy was in investment banking, and on the stock exchange and soon it would be everywhere. It was all about technology and the internet. The new economy was where the buzz was, and where the money was, if not now then certainly in the future.

The old economy was for boring people who weren't quite with the times and didn't get it. And who would be left behind by expanding profit margins and soaring stock prices. Together with their old fashioned attitudes. Who wants to be old?

To us in the Center, all this made supreme sense. After all, weren't we here because of our skills with the latest computer technology? Didn't we spend our waking nights deeply immersed in the universe of this new world? Ten years ago, oh, five years ago even, our jobs had not even existed. New technology had created them, and constantly evolved them, both inside and outside of the Bank.

Booklet after Booklet was filled with the praises of high tech companies. On the Eighth Floor, trusted Center specialists created flashy presentations, trying to capture the spirit of this new age. We did our best to jazz up the old templates, to make them look more trendy and stylish, although bankerish too, still, of course. We were still respectable. The Bank was cutting-edge and rock solid at the same time.

The logos of the high tech companies became very familiar to us. They raised millions before they even started. Some didn't even start at all. Their founders retired rich before the age of thirty. Why were we not more like them? It was hard to tell. The bankers definitely thought about it a lot, contemplating exit options but still hanging on for dear life in the face of the next cull.

I also saw those new companies when I googled at home. I looked at them and occasionally, fleetingly, I wondered why their stocks were so valuable. How exactly did they make their money? I didn't know.

'Well, obviously, they don't make any money now', said the bankers when I asked them.

'They're only starting up. It's the new economy!'

I felt stupid and didn't ask any further.

The Eighth Floor

The Seventh Floor outcrop, our mini cathedral between the Four Windows Open to the Sky, realm of despair and impermanence, cystitis, fear and swollen feet was by no means the only space occupied by the Center of Global Excellence inside the Most Successful Bank in the Universe. There were quite a few others, spread all around the building and, Rumour said, even beyond.

Like all other essential information, this was never officially revealed to me, but like all of us, I did eventually find out through informal intelligence gathering, Ilya, and close personal observation. In fact, the nearest such satellite space was directly above us on the Eighth Floor, accessible either by lift and two sets of company pass fortified glass doors or by taking the shortcut up the smokers' stairs and hoping the door was still propped open by the same battered old pack of paper.

One night, a few months into my second year, I was suddenly sent for another Test.

Not everyone, this time. Just a chosen few…

'Do exactly what they ask', whispered Coco as I passed her and her pack of carrots on my way down to the Third Basement, 'exactly. Carry out every word of the instructions. Literally.' She stretched out a hand towards the carrots and snatched it back. Her weight was steadily increasing. I was surprised that she should try to help me.

'I know', she added. 'I failed that test four times.'

I decided to take her advice. It was the same advice the agent in a coat had given me that first night. It was advice I should probably listen to a lot more.

But in the lift I remembered project 'Big Tiger' and from there it was only a heartbeat to fantasies of being fired. All the way down the basement corridors. In my mind, I had already received the call from the agency, when I sat down at the old school desk in the Training Room and opened the Test Paper.

I could hardly believe my eyes. Now I knew what the advice Coco had given me was for. What I was holding in my hands, I realised, could only be the fabled Ability Test for HEG or 'High End Graphics'. Rumour knew about it, Ilya had mentioned it (although not from personal experience), Des had of course taken it long ago when I started out on my always short shifted Saturday graveyards, but never in my wildest dreams would I have thought that I, the Grumpy Old WitchBitch, would be selected to sit the HEG Test.

Even being sent for the HEG Test was a rare and coveted distinction, and the selection process was completely obscure.

Who knew what was going on behind the impenetrable walls of S&I? They certainly never let on. And then, of course, most of those selected for the honour of taking the HEG Test failed it.

With all those thoughts running around in my head, I had a rare opportunity to experience the perfect mix of hope and futility.

It was also a nice opportunity for Des to watch me experience it as he ascended the platform of our erstwhile Trainer and told me not to hang about, most people didn't manage to even finish the HEG Test in the allocated time. He volunteered no information on his own Test.

I was exceptionally lucky that night. I didn't have the flu and I had slept for almost 12 hours. Some days I did that. I never intended to but every two weeks or so I fell into a deep well of oblivion straightaway when I came home in the morning and only woke up in time to go back to the graveyard night shift.

That night was such a night and while I always mourned a wasted day that would never come again it had given me extra clarity and an energy boost.

'You will be able to go up to the Eighth Floor, if you pass', said Ilya with ill concealed envy the following night.

Hope flared up in me again. I quickly concealed it.

'They get all the best work', he added. 'Yellow front page. Mostly long jobs, too.'

Another flare inside my stomach, this time squashed out by fear.

'Good luck.'

I thanked him. I knew he tried to mean it, and that was more than most of us managed.

Five people from the evening and night shift were Tested that week. I could see no pattern or common denominator between us. The Universe the Bank was so successful in was one of random events devoid of structure and meaning.

Of the five being Tested (another Selection of the Fittest, however random it might seem to us) down the Third

Basement, all failed, except for me.

Once again I had cheated fate.

For a short time I was tempted to believe in my own superiority. Was I not now part of an elite group with proven HEG qualities? Had I not been chosen for Better Things up on the Eighth Floor? Was I not now one of the Fittest around here? It was a strange feeling, even weirder than the Grumpy Old WitchBitch, and a lot more dangerous to my survival.

Only a month later, the Bank went on another hiring binge. Where did all the money come from for that? Not even Rumour knew.

The four failures from my HEG week were Tested once again, without any further training or advice. This time, they all passed.

Supply and demand, I supposed. I felt an urge to make cynical jokes. For a few shifts I couldn't resist sneaking around the Center, hissing 'it's a miracle' into the air whenever the shift leaders were not looking. But maybe I was just a little bit bitter because I clearly wasn't quite so superior after all. Could it be that the HEG elite was a bit of a sham?

Of course that was an observation I kept to myself. The others seemed happy.

We all did our HEG Training together.

Angel food

The Eighth Floor was quiet. I could hear it immediately, just walking up the smokers' stairs. I was so relieved I almost cried.

The inhabitants of this oasis were all rumoured to be valuable old lags most of whom I had only seen from a distance so far, Manuel, Ettore, Kitkats.

I stowed my supply bags under a readily available desk and signed in again at the new terminal. My time sheet was of course still on the Seventh Floor, under Claire's control. She had given out huge sighs of relief just behind my back at the news of my ascendance, however temporary, but I had also heard her predict my imminent and abysmal failure upstairs to her dogsbodies. That way, whatever happened, my leader was covered.

Manuel and Ettore helped me with the unfamiliar equipment so that I wouldn't be late, and Kitkats was getting coffees for all. No time deductions up here, if they could prevent it.

I felt a little disoriented. The space looked very similar to the one only a floor away, the same Four Windows on the starry Night, the same rows of desks, even a (currently empty) elevated platform for S&I.

But the atmosphere was completely different. Calm, quiet, friendly. Everybody introduced themselves with their names. As I opened up my first specialist job with the yellow front page, I realised that I didn't even want to put my music on. Compared to the Seventh Floor, it felt like a spa retreat.

Straightaway I got a very complicated chart that would have been certain death by a thousand cuts down there on the Seventh, since it was not only beyond my abilities but probably beyond Des', too. On the Eighth Floor, I didn't even try to hide it. I showed it to Manuel and he called in Ettore to help. Just like that.

Ettore, who I was given to understand was officially only an operator like the rest of us, smiled when he understood how difficult the problem was. I could see him relax (relax!) as he started to build up a series of possible scenarios. He looked as if he had put on a shoe that fit after walking all week in patent leather.

I had a hunch.

'Are you studying computer sciences?' I asked.

'Yes,' Ettore blushed. 'Part time. It'll be another two years or so.'

'And then –'

Ettore blushed even more. He really really needed to stay here, upstairs, and never come down to the Seventh Floor. Ever.

'Then I'll find a better job', he said.

'In a Better Place', I responded. I heard the others repeat

it, quietly. 'A Better Place.' Like a response in church.

'Like Peter did, you know', he said, 'I have been looking already. But it's not easy. The situation has changed. But I will, I will find something.'

He laughed apologetically.

'Of course', I said. 'Of course, of course.'

While I moved on to a juicy illustration that was almost fun to create, Ettore took the complicated graph over 'Can I? You don't mind?' and was immersed in it within the minute. He was in a Better Place already.

And so was I. The Seventh Floor, although only a few meters underneath our feet, seemed to have been left behind in a different dimension. Slowly, cautiously, I decompressed and my internal organs expanded. Slowly, I remembered. This was normality. I recognized it from memory.

Outside this new Room with the Four Windows on the Night, the antithesis of the Devil's Cathedral downstairs, the city spread towards the horizon, the stars twinkled in, and the long band of the Thames flowed through the primordial swamp, dinosaur bodies dreaming under the moon. It was a full moon that night, the colour of old bones.

After a decent interval, Manuel got up and offered another coffee round. When he got back, he brought sweets from the sweets machine for everyone. No one paid him. It was a gift, he said. I couldn't help looking over my shoulder for trouble. There was none. Only work and silence. No shouting, no humiliation games, no vicious in-fighting to suck away my energy. After a few hours I realised how much faster I was getting through my jobs, although they were much more difficult than the ones we were doing on the Seventh Floor.

It must be because I was eating angel food.

Ethan's game

I slept so well that day, after my first night on the Eighth Floor.

And the next night I was allowed to return.

Many urgent projects apparently.

Claire contented herself with smiling sardonically. She knew who would have the last laugh.

I tried to focus only on tonight.

For the first time since I entered the Most Successful Bank in the Universe I found that I was almost looking forward to my work.

Ettore, Manual and Kitkats all remembered my name. I resolved to beat them to the sweets machine. This night would be my treat.

Of course we were not completely without surveillance up here. Periodically, someone from the Seventh Floor would come up and check on us.

Instantly we snapped back into hyper vigilance. Even privileged trustees like Manuel and Kitkats anxiously checked their desk space to make sure they offered no point of attack. It was sad to see that even they were so vulnerable, but of course they were subject to the same basic rules as everyone else, such as being short shifted, culled and even individually fired for offences that would never even be named.

As for me, I felt the familiar contraction in my stomach as soon as I heard the steps of the shift leader echo in the empty work floor outside the Center. Bent low over my keyboard, I focused on producing as many mouse movements or key strokes as possible, even if it didn't really advance my current work project, and I held my breath.

Even before I heard the voice, I always could tell who it was, just by the footsteps. Just one of the skills you picked up in the Center.

Aha, Ethan tonight. I must listen out for his ever changing mood...

'All working fast, I hope', he said in a tone perfectly positioned between joking and accusation.

'Yes, yes, yes oh yes', we answered. We tried to give each other some dignity by avoiding eye contact. I felt an urge to show Ethan my big stack of finished Pages to prove my diligence but managed to resist.

'Is there a lot of work then tonight', said Kitkats.

Angelic atmosphere or not, the workload still determined

our nightly income.

Ethan could feel our tension too, and he wasn't going to relieve it. I couldn't help looking up, as did all the others, one by one, until we all stared at him, please tell us, please let us know how much you will let us get paid tonight, less than last week, more than last week, will we get our full eight hours, will we get six, will we get four, or will there be overtime?

Ethan said nothing. He came over and sat down next to us in the row of work desks. Eye to eye. Man to man.

Ethan of course sometimes did things like that. Not in Claire's presence, where he was very circumspect, only when she couldn't see him. He was careful to be, sometimes, a man of the people and to draw a subtle distinction between himself and the worst excesses downstairs. I felt he was investing in a kind of two ways insurance, just in case. As it turned out, this strategy would serve him well in the future.

On the other hand, he knew where to draw the line. In all the time I knew him, he never once had a dispute with S&I. His integration with them was seamless. This also turned out to be to his advantage later.

'Will you be asking us to stay on', said Manuel. I knew he was trying to be stoic about life's little trials because he had told us. Face fate fair and square was his philosophy.

Ethan let the question hang in the air, making sure that we all understood that he didn't have to answer at all if he didn't feel like it.

'Yes', he said finally, 'I probably will, but not all of you.'

Mission achieved, he turned and left. His footsteps echoed all the way to the glass doors. I wished I could follow him and go to the toilet, but my next eye break was still almost an hour away.

Just as the shift leaders and managers suspected, no keyboard stroke or mouse click was to be heard as soon as these footsteps receded.

I put my head down and started to redo all the mistakes I had made during Ethan's control visit.

Kitkats took her hands off the keyboard and stretched her arms out towards the ceiling.

'What would you do if you won the lottery?' she said.

'I'm going to make a list with the most unusual answers', said Ettore, excel sheet at the ready.

'I would just make sure that everybody is ok', said Manuel, 'my children, my wife. I would take them all on a visit to Argentina. I would just carry on.'

'I would buy another house', said Kitkats. 'Do it up, then sell it on. My boyfriend is really into this. He says we're going to retire early.'

'I'd set up a startup', said Ettore. 'I've got lots of ideas…'

A bit of silence, then they asked. 'And you?'

'If I won the lottery, I would tell no one', I heard myself say. 'No one at all.'

Back down to the Seventh

Unfortunately, but not unexpectedly, my ascendance to the Eighth Floor was never permanent.

I never found out why, but I always remained only a guest up there, and my returns to the Seventh, sometimes within the same shift, were as painful as the time spent upstairs was precious. Life never lost its sharp edges. Not for me, and not in the Bank.

Song of the Sweets Machine 2

The naughtiest sweet of them all was a wafer drenched in chocolate candy. When you bit into it, the wafer crunched, and the candy dissolved. It was a little too hard and too cold when it came out of the machine. I knew that because I never waited for it to reach room temperature. I couldn't. Just stuffed it in. Machine to mouth. Gone by the time I made it back to the desk.

Sometimes, usually in summer, a wafer with special flavour came out. One year it was orange. The other year it was mint. Kitkats on the Eighth Floor remembered them all.

People are so isolated in London

'People are so isolated in London', Claire said. 'It's a disgrace. I hardly know my neighbours.'

I reached over to turn my Page, taking great care not to knock over Coco's scientifically arranged stacks of rice cakes and oranges and at the same time avoiding elbow contact with my other neighbour. I surreptitiously tried to exercise my ankles under the desk but was hampered by the fact that I had only managed to get a flimsy plastic footrest at the start of the shift.

'Yes, I think it's such a shame', Coco agreed. I was sure she had her extra wide feet on the good iron footrest that I coveted. 'People used to be so much closer to each other, in the past.'

More agreement throughout the room.

I thought how much I wanted that iron footrest. It made your toes look up and your heels look down. My feet had started to swell up quite dramatically at the end of every shift, and the footrest really made a lot of difference by improving circulation.

'People were so much closer to each other in the villages, in the countryside, you know, they just had to get on with each other, and they did', said Ethan. So he didn't just read management magazines, did he, he also seemed to know his way around Country Life. Of course I couldn't say that, but even the thought helped.

Catherine came back from her eye break, as always sticking her head round the corner first like some long necked bird, ready to withdraw at the first sign of danger. When she got to my desk, she whispered into my shoulder.

'Don't you think it's cold?'

I was back to thinking about Deep Vein Thrombosis. Trapped in my chair for eight hours, wasn't I likely to develop similar symptoms as someone on a long haul flight? (Particularly if I didn't have a proper footrest…)

When I didn't respond she rubbed her hands together in a pitiful manner.

But I couldn't really say anything. On the Seventh Floor I had to preserve my WitchBitch persona.

'It's the air condition', said Claire. 'I've always said it. Call the engineers.'

The dogsbodies laughed. Catherine coughed.

'It's got the dirt of twelve years inside its pipes', said Coco. Had she been here that long? 'Did you see what happened when they took the panel off?'

I realised I was holding my breath. For a good few seconds, thanks to my expensive Yoga classes. Then I succumbed in a great shivering sigh. My head sagged against my head rest. I jerked it up again.

The headrests were provided by the Bank on the advice of a health expert who had trained us one morning in the best way of sitting at a desk. Excessive sitting, she said, was just as damaging to the body as extreme sports. I could well believe it. The evidence was in my feet.

Unfortunately the headrests (that also made a big difference) were detachable and regularly ripped out by reckless operators who threw them on the dirty carpet where the lice and the tea stains were. So then I had a choice between spinal deterioration and skin infections.

'I have the number', said Claire generously, pointing to the wall above the Front Desk where a lot of posties and sheets of all sizes and colours hung in colourful chaos.

'I hope they don't turn the air off completely', said Des, joining the conversation from his great height, 'like they did last time. I was suffocating.'

'I suppose if we all produced carbon dioxide all night and there was no inflow of oxygen we would die', said Ethan slowly.

At that moment, just I was re-immersing myself in my scatter chart, yellow dots flying across my screen like the signs of the financial Zodiac, the background humming stopped.

'The air condition is off', said Ethan, just to help out the deaf.

'I'm getting a headache', said Des, snapping his pill case open.

'Better a headache than the killer virus', said Claire, and then laughed uproariously, to show that she was in no way being disrespectful to S&I.

People returned to their work, breathing in the remaining oxygen, puffing out carbon dioxide. Silently, they shed hairs, droplets of sweat, tiny flakes of their skin.

Almost silently, the terminals connected with their servers, and with the overall operations control in New York.

4 o'clock struck, and many people, those that were not on diets and therefore had to eat rice cakes and half green oranges and twice a night desperate life savers from the sweets machine, got out their dinners and started the race to the microwave. My useless plastic footrest collapsed onto itself.

5 o'clock came, deadlines approaching all over the globe. Around me the clicking of keyboards and the breathing of mammals. And the slow running out of life times.

'People are so isolated in London', said Claire.

Song of the Sweets Machine 3

And you I keep for last, you nasty little Number Seven. The Devil's Number. Very apt.

Number Seven holds the portals of hell wide open. It has no chocolate, no nuts, no oil. No redeeming feature whatsoever. Number Seven is a roll of gelatine, gelatine that is the fat underneath a cow's skin, saturated in sugar, boiled, cut into red and black slices coloured with additives so toxic that it takes nearly half of the wrapper to list them in font size two (and I knew all about font size two – it's unreadable without a microscope).

My favourites were the black slices. They left the devil's mark on my tongue and I craved them every night.

Number Seven is the sweet of my despair.

Graveyard remix

As I tumbled out of the small nondescript door, the

graveyard lay in a white mist, not quite thick enough to obscure the tombstones, but whispy enough to soften their dark edges. If you held your head at a certain angle and squinted a bit you could pretend you were somewhere in the countryside where such a scenery could be the setting for a romantic walk. Or a post card.

My swollen feet carried my exhausted body along the well trodden path next to John Ambersand's grave. I stopped for a moment, saluting his brief life and terrible death from the plague, and then I remembered.

Today was the day.

And that meant I couldn't go home.

The lady on the phone had given me a 10 o'clock appointment. I knew she meant to be kind, ignoring my protests that I could easily come earlier.

'No, no', she said and wouldn't hear of it.

So I was now faced with the notorious graveyard gap, having to kill time at the end of my day so that I could meet someone at the start of theirs.

But it was in a good cause: the final interview for admission to my course! If successful, I would finally embark on my journey to a Better Place. I would also have find ways to regularly bridge the graveyard gap…

I retreated a little deeper into the graveyard, but not too close to the crypt, since I now knew what was inside. Then I sat on a tomb and idly watched life go by. It was alright, because today I had somewhere to go. The cold from the stone seeped into my thighs. That was ok too. It reminded me of other moments in the graveyard that took on an almost nostalgic glow in retrospect. I had been so innocent, walking into this trap… But then, I did need the money. I needed it still, and would, more than ever, if I was accepted today. And then again, just look what money can do…

Through the lifting mist, another romantic filter that made me think of old paintings and old movies, I saw a few of my colleagues pass the tombs on their way to the street and then, who knew where else. Away. Intent on leaving the night behind, no one turned. Nobody saw me.

A bunch of morning bankers trampled in the opposite direction. I watched them stand and impatiently curse at the door, then disappear inside in a great hurry, pushing each other aside just a little too hard but laughing loudly enough that I could hear them.

Most of the bankers used the grander entrance on the other side of course, and most of them arrived in Bank paid taxis before eating their Bank paid breakfasts and filling up on coffee at the Bank's in-house premium brand coffee shop.

The door opened again and this time I saw a group of our Seventh Floor newbies stagger out. I wasn't surprised they were late. They had probably been held behind after sign-out to look at their mistakes and repent. The newbies blinked in the timid daylight and took a while to orient themselves. One or two groggily held onto the headstones. Now I wished I had retreated deeper into the graveyard, crypt or not. The coffins couldn't accost me.

One of the guys took out a pack of cigarettes and huddled next John Ambersand's grave to light up. Somehow I didn't like that. John Ambersand felt like a family friend by now.

The others walked off one by one, losing themselves and each other in the traffic where they would be just like anyone else.

The smoker sucked on his nicotine stick and looked round, as smokers will. And waved. He wasn't waving at me, was he? I looked down at the grass and at my by now not-so-new shoes, the first ones I had bought with the Bank's money. These shoes wouldn't last much longer. Then I would need new ones, which meant more money, which meant hoping for good news on the ATM slips, which meant getting as many full shifts as possible, which meant not getting fired… I should really stop worrying and instead prepare for my interview. Attitude! A positive attitude will always impress. So something had stuck in my mind from all those self help books…

'Hi Nyla', said a voice close to my head.

Startled, I shrunk back on my tomb.

For a nano second I thought I had heard Peter's voice, surprising me in a similar fashion that afternoon during our

Basic Training, now almost two years ago.

Then I looked up. Of course it wasn't Peter, it was the smoker.

Puffing on his cigarette and wiping his feet on something sticky.

'Hi', I said. But not with a lot of enthusiasm.

He looked hurt.

I should be nice, I told myself. I had seen what they did to him on the Seventh Floor. His life was hard enough. But somehow I wasn't in the mood. I needed to focus on myself right now.

'I've got to go', I said, gathering my bags.

The smoker gave a short, bitter laugh as if I had just confirmed his low opinion of me. Well, I had been rude, by the standards of the outside world. On the other hand, his reaction seemed a bit over the top. Almost as if he had just come off a night shift... But it was probably all for the best, considering the WitchBitch persona I needed to keep up on the Seventh Floor.

He threw his cigarette butt down and tried to grind it into the grass.

Rude or not, I was on the point of saying something when I realised what the sticky thing was that clung to his shoe.

While we were up maximising shareholder value in the Building Without a Name, death had come to one of the numerous rodents that lived in this graveyard and this city, a death just as wild as it would be anywhere in the countryside. What could be more natural? Predators kill their prey! And the smoker had just trodden on its corpse.

I looked up at the sky but the predator was hiding somewhere, waiting until we, superior predators, moved away.

The smoker had also noticed what he had stepped in. 'This is disgusting', he said.

'It's life', I said. And managed a little smile.

Then I waved and walked away.

Far be it from me to deny a predator his breakfast.

The Smiler

The following graveyard shift was a full return to the Seventh Floor at its worst.

I had already been shunted to a seat right underneath the broken air vent, given the fag end of a job that had been handed down three shifts (so that the original instructions were now lost in the mists of time and mistakes unavoidable) and had witnessed what looked like an alarming uptick of pressure on the latest bunch of newbies (including the smoker from last morning who pretended he couldn't see me – what a waste of a smile).

And now, for the last two hours, I had been hit with the fate that was worse than death, 'sitting with the banker', but this time not in the Center. I had been sent to work with him out in the Field of Desks.

This particular banker was so notorious that I almost knew his name. Almost, because we had our own name for him in the Center. He was a little higher up the chain than a mere analyst, and Claire had recently lost a few battles with him. That was unusual, and it was also the reason why I was now squashed into a corner of his cross. Claire was making sure that any future losses would not be hers.

And it was part of my punishment for having been selected to do HEG on the Eighth Floor earlier this week.

This banker was toxic as black gelatine. We called him 'The Smiler'. He hardly let my bum hit the extra chair squashed in beside his before he accused me of holding up the proceedings with my lazy attitude. Then I had to stare at the screen for many minutes while he subjected me to a comprehensive presentation of his creative concept.

Being higher up, the Smiler had acquired some underlings of his own who had been kept in the office night after night as long as he was there, and sometimes longer. They were here right now, surrounding the desk and hanging on the Smiler's every word. They agreed with everything he said him, nodding vigorously and giving me dirty looks. They also eagerly volunteered to perform the most menial of tasks –

and I discovered soon that their eagerness increased when those tasks took them elsewhere. I didn't have that option. I had to sit in the squashed chair.

Smiling, the banker went on to educate me in high end graphics (or, as we called it, HEG), a subject he was sadly misinformed on, pausing at regular intervals to extort a yes from me. I told myself that at least I didn't have to call him Sir. Luckily I was by now an expert at agreeing with things I hadn't listened to. If I argued with him it would only take longer, and I would be blamed for the delay. If I did it his way I would be blamed too but at least I would have the satisfaction of seeing his instructions tank miserably and mess up the Page (before I fixed it unobtrusively). My goal was to leave him and his toxic Smiles behind as soon as possible and re-unite with the Sweets Machine.

In the distance, the silhouettes of bankers were moving around like a Javanese shadow play, clustering together and drifting apart again. From time to time there was an outbreak of shouting and papers flew in the air. Occasionally an operator hurried to the kitchen.

My banker went on talking, smiling all the way. Maybe I should just look on this as an unofficial break… The longer he talked, the longer I didn't actually have to do anything. My mind wandered, and so did my gaze…

Suddenly, my breath caught.

What had happened?

It wasn't the banker. He was still safely droning on about pixellation and perspective. And none of his minions had come back. There was no movement in the vicinity of our cross.

I scanned the shadowy shapes in the distance again, the way my ancestors had scanned the twilight savannah.

Suddenly, but very briefly, my heart faltered in its neverending duty.

There! Somewhere in the cluster of shades at the end of the Field. I watched that cluster more closely. It moved and shifted, flowed back and forth, contracted for a moment and then dissolved into the distinct shapes of separate figures.

One of these shapes wavered for a moment and then moved towards the Center.

Blood rushed through my ears so that I could no longer hear the banker's opinions on fade-through transitions.

The shape had almost reached the narrow entrance to the Room with the Four Windows on the Night. As it crossed over the dark threshold, it turned a little to the side and the last light from the Field of Desks fell across its face.

Peter.

Peter was Back.

'Be creative', said the banker, 'you know what I want.'

He crossed his arms over his suit, crumpled now but worth at least five hundred pounds more than the suits of his underlings who had reluctantly returned and were trying to look invisible and busy at the same time.

The Smiler leaned back and smiled, preparing to supervise my every movement and question my every decision.

Peter Comes Back

Back? How could Peter be Back? He alone, out of all of us, was the one who would make it. He wouldn't waste his life between the Four Windows. He would get a big bucks job in IT. And then, who knew what else…

What did this mean? My head was spinning superwebs, trying to reconstruct my model of the universe.

The Smiler was very disappointed in me, he said.

He'd had to repeat himself several times and I clearly was incapable of grasping the concept of HEG. It looked to him almost as if I wasn't really there.

For once, the banker was right although of course he didn't know it.

Peter was Back.

What did I feel? Testing my weight on swollen feet, I couldn't decide. I felt so many things at the same time.

I hardly knew you...

The following night I was standing in the sign up queue on the Seventh Floor, squashed between Coco and a few newbies, already under heavy barrage from Des for 'letting the banker down last night', and fully prepared to deploy the WitchBitch.

But I got a lucky break. The work load was still very heavy, the Yellow Front Sheet Jobs were literally falling off the Front Desk and so, with a sigh, Claire let me out of her clutches, told me to pick one up, and sent me up to the Eighth Floor. 'But no slacking and only until that job is finished!' she shouted after me. I nodded and picked up my backpack. As I turned I saw someone slouching towards the end of the queue. Peter.

I could now see his face more clearly than from all the way across the work floor last night – he looked sick. His eyes had a feverish glimmer and dark rings underneath and his skin was dull. His formerly trim body was developing a premature paunch. He walked with a stoop and from time to time he winced, like someone with a hidden wound.

What on earth had happened to him?

All I could tell right now was that these changes didn't look as if they were the result of spending too much time in a Better Place.

I hesitated to speak to him, since he gave no sign of recognising me. Maybe I, too, had changed more than I realised...

Safe in the silence of the Eighth Floor, I felt sorry for him.

Of course, I felt sorry for him.

On the other hand, the memory of the disregarded phone number pushed itself into the forefront of my mind. I could see that number right now, the many twists of my crumpled paper, his indifferent expression as he took it.

When I was sent back down from the Eighth Floor a few hours later, I saw that Peter had been put into the front row, right next to the front desk. Des had his screen in view, and Claire was constantly walking up to him and looking over his shoulder, now and then shooting out an arm to point out a mistake. Next to him sat Ethan, on an operator shift. Nowhere to go, no place to escape. From time to time Peter frantically clicked on a webflash. Then Claire reminded him that we didn't take breaks here. 'And you don't get up!' she added.

The newbies hung their heads. They knew this routine all too well.

I was able to get one of the better seats at the back. From there I reflected on the strange twists of fate, or the Most Successful Bank in the Universe. Compared to Peter, I now had privilege in the Center. I got long jobs, some of them yellow. I didn't have to show my work except in the regular quality control crack downs, and I even got spend semi-unsupervised time on the Eighth Floor with the HEG trustees.

Peter, on the other hand, I heard in a whisper from Paulo and later saw on a webflash from Catherine, was now officially a newbie again and was 'working towards his three month assessment'.

Wow.

The night dragged on, long hours until sunlight. My job was boring and demanding in equal parts. I squeezed tiny pie charts into shrinking spaces, I adjusted headlines (always down, the bankers had learnt nothing) and expertly created layouts. I played my favourite track from the Lord of the Rings on my one earphone.

Peter was not so lucky. Claire selected his Pages. She reminded him to hand in the finished ones to Des ('You remember Des? He used to be an operator when you left and – look at him now! Hahaha!') to check. He trotted over to her, eyes on the floor.

'Petey', Skinney called out to him. She was testing how much she was allowed to do. A lot, it seemed. Particularly considering that she hadn't been here all that long. Laughter from the first row, elevated and ordinary, greeted her witty remark. Claire winked at her. Des approved.

I watched as Peter sagged further into his clothes, hesitated for a moment, and then obeyed.

'Hi Petey', said Des. 'Let's see what you've got.'

Peter was Back?

'He couldn't make it you know', said Manuel softly, into the silence of the Eighth Floor. 'Such a pity.'

I wondered why. Peter was clever, and confident, and flexible. And, as far as I knew, determined to reach his goal.

'I don't want to talk about it', said Ettore, blushing again, but this time it looked painful.

In the sign out queue Ettore nearly ran into Peter, and suddenly drew back, letting a few others fill the gap between them. The queue was extra slow tonight because Claire and Des were analysing the moral and physical flaws of the most recent batch and that was going to take a while. We had to wait to get Claire's signature without which we wouldn't be paid and usually everyone tried to cut ahead if they got the chance. Natural selection down to the last second. But to Ettore, who was still pursuing his own IT course, Peter was one of the walking dead.

I still couldn't quite believe the evidence of my ears and eyes.

Peter? Peter was Back?

Peter in the kitchen

And then, deep into the next night on the Seventh Floor, as I was standing guard over the microwave, three minute soup inside and hand on the door, ready for crisis intervention, I felt a shadow move behind me. Anticipating trouble, I turned.

It was Peter, leaning against the kitchen door.

I didn't know what to say.

He looked at me blankly, then lifted the corners of his mouth for a second before letting them go slack again.

That made me bold.

'Hi Peter', I said. 'What a surprise.'

'Yes', he said, looking at me sideways from his dark shaded eyes, 'I didn't think I would come back either.'

'No…', I said. What else was there to say? Well, a lot actually, but it was all on his side.

'It was the best thing I could do', Peter said, looking down. Where the only thing he could see was the overflowing rubbish bin.

The best thing? Really? The Center the best thing? What on earth could that mean?

Peter looked up and said earnestly: 'I need the money.'

Somehow that made me angry. 'Yes, me too', I said.

Peter sighed.

I took a step forward and looked him in the eye. 'Peter', I said, 'what happened to you? Out there?'

Peter said nothing. He looked down again.

He shifted his weight against the door frame and leaned on the lid of the rubbish bin. The lid wouldn't close because the bin was too full. Peter pushed some more. But all he achieved was to make it even more crooked.

To my own surprise I heard myself say: 'Are you alright? Can I help you in some way?'

Peter's face seemed to light up a little bit.

I was pleased.

How quickly that happened. Peter smiled and I was pleased. Pleased little dumped phone number I told myself. Be careful!

'Yes', Peter continued, 'I've had some rough times.'

He shoved the lid down with such force that he actually managed to press it almost to the rim of the bin. I suddenly wondered how rough exactly those times had been.

'Lost my apartment, just before the final exam.' He hit the lid once more. A thick brown clump of something fell out of the far side of the bin. Peter jumped away.

I shrank back towards the microwave.

The thick brown clump lay in the kitchen corner, just shy

of the sweets machine. When it didn't move, our eyes met.

I couldn't help it. I smiled. Peter smiled back. Much more broadly now.

Once again, I could feel the familiar pull. Peter was here. And I had seen a shadow of his old smile… At the same time I couldn't help thinking about my soup in the microwave. Hopefully everything was ok there.

'And my girlfriend left me…'

Oh! That brought my attention back. Sharp and fast.

Oh, oh.

A splutter from the microwave. Then a bang.

My soup had boiled over and flooded the whole oven. When I reached in, the spill was already thickening into an angry red crust. Only a little puddle of thick liquid would be left at the bottom of my plastic bowl for me to eat (if I was lucky) but who cared. Peter had lost his girlfriend.

'I'm sorry to hear that', I lied. Mopping the microwave with flimsy tissues.

He nodded. In a manner appropriate to the seriousness of his suffering.

A brown liquid had now started to ooze out of the rubbish bin. With more bits in it. Bits that had been food at some point. Before they had been digested by the Seventh Floor kitchen bin…

'I can tell you more about it, if you like', he said softly.

'Petey!' That was Skinney passing.

Peter's head jerked over to her, but then he defiantly leaned into the door again.

'Well if you want to come out for coffee some time after work…', he said, very calmly now, very much in command of his voice, as if he had not been interrupted at all.

Peter was asking me out?

'Well you have my phone number', I said. I couldn't resist it.

He didn't even look guilty. Suddenly I noticed that he hadn't actually called me by my name. Maybe he had forgotten what it was?

'Well', Peter said. 'I moved house… twice…'

He shrugged and smiled again, quite brilliantly. That

smile… 'I really have to go.'

That much at least was true. Skinney was cruising.

I christened the occasion with burnt tomato remnants. Roasted red, not unattractive, sticky and sweetly crumbling underneath.

So, yes. It seemed that Peter was Back.

WitchBitch and friends

The rest of the night went by in a flash.

I sat and worked, protected by my food, books, music and WitchBitch persona. Although Claire, I was sure, had sensed something. She lifted her head as I walked by, almost as if she could smell the change. Or maybe, like a spider, she was able to respond to variations in body temperature and hormone levels. Or maybe it was just the way I carried my bowl of burnt tomato residue and the spring in my step as I took a long a tedious pink job back to my desk and didn't even roll my eyes when it was fished out from under two more desirable ones that had clearly been earmarked for Skinney and another rising collaborator.

Other people, luckily, were not so sensitive. They felt no sparks in the air and continued to discuss their home re-financing plans with their backs turned, just as they always did when the WitchBitch passed.

I knew where Peter was sitting, and I was so tempted! But I didn't look. Couldn't look. If I did, I would endanger him, and I would also endanger myself.

Looking around I saw the familiar spectacle of a newbie being humiliated. A tall young man rumoured to be an out of work actor was standing in front of the elevated S&I desks. Des was not nearly as tall as the actor but managed to tower over him by a few centimetres with the aid of the platform. At the same time, Des leant backwards at an exaggerated angle and wrinkled his nose. This was a relatively new variant in the game but I already knew why. Des had announced the reason every night since the young actor joined, as soon as he was out of the room. The actor Smelled.

The actor (Jeff?) was saying something and was then asked to speak up. He did, in loud and ringing tones. Was he mocking S&I? Maybe not. Maybe he couldn't help sounding Shakespearian while he promised that he would look at his best practices and try to do better next time. Des' head hit the wall behind him – this was as far as he could go – and handed the actor his faulty sheets with the furthest ends of his fingertips.

The scene was familiar but that didn't mean it had lost its effect.

No. No way. No way could I give up my WitchBitch protection. I moved my music device closer to my keyboard and sighed loudly when Paulo, trapped in the corner seat between the West and North Windows, tried to push past my chair on his way to the toilet.

But no one could control how I felt inside. Inside I was singing along sweetly with my new collection of Alison Krauss.

Peter was Back.

No room in the Better Place

Peter was not the only one who had run into trouble.

Ilya had stopped his part time course a few months ago.

'Just too much for me', he said. 'And then what's the point. My wife agrees. What's the point of killing myself if I only have to Come Back?'

'Peter says he's only here temporarily', said Catherine. 'He says he's still looking for a better job.'

A sad little smile crossed Ilya's face.

When I thought about it, so far, I hadn't actually heard of anyone who had definitely been successful in their quest of going to a Better Place. Of course it could just be because the ones who had truly been successful wouldn't make contact with us. They would want to forget.

The shadows of Mordor

Peter might have lost everything but he had given me what I wanted. A date.

A date with Peter in the coffeeshop. Before I even knew it, my mind had called it that.

Finally, I would sit with Peter in the coffeeshop (and I resolved there and then that it had to be the posh one with the red sofa and the logo from our first encounter in the graveyard) and have him all to myself. After all, he had lost his girlfriend, hadn't he. Through no fault of mine.

And his skin, while a little dulled perhaps, was still pale and smooth. With a promise of softness.

It wasn't a date, I told myself sternly, racing through my job with the speed of a high oestrogen train, it was just a get-together, a conversation (my mind shied away from the word 'chat' which had acquired a somewhat ominous meaning in the Center) with an old friend. Yes, that was already a given. We were friends. Old friends.

And I would find out why he had come Back.

My mind raced ahead, scouting out possibilities. Especially about those rough times and what he did after he lost his flat...

And I had other things to think of, too.

I had been accepted into the course I had applied for. The lady had been most kind on the phone. Apparently my attitude that morning had not failed to convince.

A lot of things were about to change.

I remembered that it could feel good to be alive.

This was perhaps why I didn't realise the full significance of her arrival although I distinctly remember the night it happened. Later I tried to pinpoint the date, the month, the season. But I couldn't. My mind was as misty on that matter as our graveyard in winter. All I remembered was that it was around the time when Peter came Back.

Vera's arrival in the Center was the beginning of our time

of terror, our collective trip to Mordor, a time that still makes my whole body shake when I think about it, a time that forced me to confront myself like never before. Mordor took my heart and wrenched it open.

But right then, if you had asked me then who of all the people in the Most Successful Bank in the Universe was likely to be the most important to me, I would of course have said Peter.

I couldn't have been more wrong.

The person who would have the most impact on my life in the Center, and also away from it, was not Peter. It was Vera.

But on that first night, I didn't feel the wings of fate approaching, I didn't see the shadow of the coming storm.

Vera

Ilya moved slowly, and picked up his keys so clumsily that they slipped from his grasp and got stuck somewhere in the back of the iron chair. I waited while he fiddled with them. His problem, not mine.

Most of the desk was covered by the keyboard and mouse pad, and the monitor, balanced high on stacked packs of paper (the packs of paper had been recommended by the sitting instructor as a low cost (and low tech) option of getting the monitors up to eye level, since the Bank obviously didn't have the resources to provide ergonomically safe equipment for us). I unpacked quickly and abundantly, leaving Ilya nowhere to go but his departing bag.

Finally, and after I retrieved his keys for him after all (the time delay had now made it into my problem alright), he slunk off.

I slipped into the seat at 00:07 precisely and took possession.

As the machine was powering up to digest my impossibly complicated password, I looked covertly at the 'S&I' platform. Des again. He seemed to be getting all my shifts. Surely that was a coincidence?

I was ready to be in a good mood again (secretly, of

course, and on the inside only). Peter was sitting in the second row, looking very miserable. He turned his job over and over as if he was looking for better news somewhere. Well, that better news was on its way. Yesterday he had finally suggested a day for our coffeeshop meetup. All that remained to make it happen was my acceptance.

Should I send him a webflash now or later, when Des was otherwise occupied?

Or should I wait until it was almost break times? I wanted to watch Peter's face at the exact moment when he got my flash. Maybe it would be fun to delay that pleasure just a little bit longer...

Yes, I had the freedom to entertain myself with such idle thoughts. But not for long...

Because then I heard the commotion at the front desk.

This was not just the usual midnight mayhem with huge dropoffs of work that needed to be completed by morning (including quite a few of the coveted all-nighters) and contests of iron will between Claire and the bankers, resulting in longer and longer queues behind the warring factions.

Claire had dealt with all that and was now standing still, looking at something just outside the Center. She sniffed the air like a blood hound. Her lips quivered. After a few moments, she started to make little abrupt movements with her hands which I suddenly realised were signals to Des. Skinney stretched up so she could see and Ethan unwrapped his sandwich.

And then it began.

A tall young woman with dark red hair, strong and competent maybe in the outside world, but a little apprehensive now, walked right into the middle of the entrance. She stopped, looking disoriented, not realising that she was blocking secret currents and undercurrents trying to stream around her. There was an openness and softness in the way she looked at us that we didn't encounter much in the Center. She was new and you could see it.

'And what might you think you are doing?' I could easily distinguish the sharpness of Claire's voice among all the complex layers of sound covering the entrance way. Well, I could by now distinguish Claire's voice in any mood and at any distance. If she was the blood hound, I was the rabbit.

The newcomer had caught onto that sharpness too, it seemed. She looked at Claire, startled and not quite sure if she had heard correctly. Her reaction startled me, in turn, out of my many months of acclimation to this kind of tone. It was not often heard in the outside world. I suddenly remembered that.

The two women locked eyes, and a dreamy expression came over Claire's angular features as she took in the newcomer's softness. The newcomer's expression changed, too, and for a moment it seemed as if she was going to cry, there and then. Surely not so quickly? At such little provocation? I didn't want to imagine how this young woman would cope with a whole shift. And then another. And another. Next to me, Paulo edged his magazine out from under his keyboard. He was right, this was a good moment for illegal activities at the back.

Claire brought her pen down sharply on the desk and the newcomer swayed a little, as if her centre of gravity had been disturbed.

'Come here', said Claire and the other woman advanced, as if drawn on a hook deep inside her flesh.

'Start at 00:30', Claire intoned. The newcomer looked confused. It was barely quarter past. And she was probably late because she, just like me on my first night up, had gotten lost in the huge Field of Desks that covered the work floor. I remembered that there was so much she hadn't been told.

Well, she was going to find out. Claire's way.

The red haired woman clutched her time sheet and turned to look for a seat. Nobody made eye contact, much less talked to her. I put my earphone in and focused on my work. She sat down right in front of S&I and tried to log on. I really didn't want to see what would happen when she called Des for help.

Maybe Vera's arrival was only the trigger to an inevitable cataclysm. Something started that night that stirred Claire and Des (and behind them, Ethan and Skinney and the various dogsbodies) into a feeding frenzy that they themselves would soon no longer be able to control, something that made them increase the pressure inside our little night cooker to a thousand delirious degrees. Maybe Claire was going wherever she was going anyway and Vera's presence only crystallised and accelerated the process. Or maybe it was Vera herself who caused it after all.

But whatever it was, and I have thought about it countless times, going over that memory from her first night, from the moment she entered the Center, when the world as she knew it ceased to exist and she crossed over into our darkness, Vera's fate was sealed.

And although I kept my head down, I was there all the way.

Yes

'Yes.'

That was all.

Peter had shown no reaction when I shot off my webflash to him. I had observed him closely. Or as closely as I could. I couldn't see his face behind the monitor, but surely there was involuntary body language when someone was surprised…

Had he always been this guarded?

I felt stupid now for delaying my answer. Careful of the mood swings on the graveyard shift!

So tomorrow morning I would wait for him in the coffee shop. On the red sofa, under the golden picture frame. He would time his own departure to make it look random. Whatever else had changed, we hadn't given up our old habit of splitting up to deceive the predators.

And then would find out why Peter had really come Back.

Monsters Arising

Sometimes, even now, I wish that Vera had never entered the Room with the Four Windows on the Night.

That she had never passed her initial Test down in the Third Basement.

That she had never applied for the job, had never found the agency in the Georgian mansion behind the Bank of England that supplied us to the Bank.

Sometimes I wish I had never met her.

She wouldn't have missed out on anything. She would have had a normal life.

And so would I.

But it was already too late for that.

While I was re-doing my hair in front of the mirror in the ladies' toilet and putting on a fresh shirt (but in the same colour) (with a new layer of deodorant underneath) to meet Peter (would he wear his cologne for me?), Vera was swimming in a circle of blood.

As she herself would later say, the Monsters were Arising.

ABOUT THE AUTHOR

Nyla Nox lives an exciting double life. She has been writing articles on the (in)-human side of banking for many years, particularly about the lives of jobless humanities graduates who are forced to serve the richest bankers in the world. Her unique knowledge of this extremely secretive world is the inspiration for the 'Graveyards of the Banks trilogy' or the 'The War and Peace of Investment Banking' as Nyla likes to call it.

'Graveyards of the Banks' is based on Nyla's real life experience at the Most Successful Bank in the Universe (not its real name), where very few outsiders have ever set foot.

Nyla also writes stories about fantastical creatures and imaginary futures. Her work has been included in numerous collections. Her articles appear in Business Insider, Open Democracy, mergers&inquisitions and efinancialcareers where they were translated into German, French and Mandarin.

Read all about Nyla's world at http://www.nylanox.com.

Graveyards of the Banks
Volume 1 – I did it for the Money
Volume 2 – Monsters Arising
Volume 3 – Slaughterhouse Morning

Printed in Great Britain
by Amazon